LUTHER

BarbarianSpy

FOR LITERARY HEAT

www.BarbarianSpy.com

This book is copyright © habu 2012
Published by BarbarianSpy in 2012
Cover design © S Bush 2012
Cover image: © Curaphotography | Dreamstime.com
ISBN 978-1-921879-33-3
All rights reserved

LUTHER

by

HABU

TABLE OF CONTENTS

CHAPTER ONE: THE SPELL OF THE BIG ONE

"Hi ya," Mr. Leighton.

Rob Leighton looked up from helping his daughter, Muriel, climb up onto the dock from his fishing boat and waved at the tall, lumbering young man walking south on Lafayette Street back toward Cape May proper.

"Hi to you, too, big guy," Rob called back. "Hot day. You have to walk all the way back to the antique shop? If so, maybe we can give you a lift." He looked around with a questioning look at his wife, Madge, who was about to hand the younger daughter, Maia, up to her husband on the dock. She was frowning slightly, but she nodded her head imperceptibly.

"Naw, thanks, Mr. Leighton. Only going as far as the house. The bosses didn't want me at the shop today. They were getting some china in and said I was needed to do something at the house."

Rob could almost hear Madge let out a breath of relief.

"Well, you be careful now," Rob called back. "If that's where Tim and Alfred want you to be, guess you should be there."

"It's OK. They said I could come and see the whale-watching boat come in. I like that boat. I like your boat too. It's—"

"That's good to hear, Luther. The *Spirit of Cape May* is a nice boat. We've got to get the girls back to the house now. It's been nice talking to you."

Luther stood there, big feet on strong legs planted firmly on the Lafayette sidewalk separated from the Cape May Harbor wharf by a parking lot where Rob and Madge were now bundling their daughters and Rob's fishing gear into an old station wagon. The young man's jaw was working like he wanted to say something else but couldn't think what it was—and thought that maybe it was something he shouldn't say. He swayed a bit back and forth, at least in front of Rob's wife and his daughters. He didn't want Mr. Leighton to be mad at him.

As the station wagon drove away, Madge looked at Rob, started to say something, seemed to think better of it, but then did speak. "I'm sorry to say I'm glad he didn't take the ride, Rob. He frightens me."

"He's harmless, Madge. And he's a good kid; he means well."

"He isn't a kid anymore, Rob. Something needs to be done about him. He's a young man now, and he's nearly on his own. What's going to happen when he gets older? He can't cope. And there's been talk. I don't want the girls—"

"The talk is just because he's always been slow, Madge. And he's so big. Tim and Alfred have taken him on at the antique shop and have let him live in those rooms behind the workshop behind their house. He's being taken care of. I think he's coping just fine."

"Tim and Alfred are hardly the influence anyone would want for that young man. If his mother were still alive—"

"She's not alive, though, is she? And she probably was too protective of him. Someone should have been working with him from the time he was young. But she wouldn't let anyone near him. I don't think he's even that retarded. Just slow. He'll be OK."

"Well, all the same, I'm just as glad we didn't have him in the car with the girls," Madge said. She crossed her arms tightly on her chest. "And mark my words, something's going to come to a head with that young man. I don't like some of the rumors I've heard. Not at all."

As the station wagon drove past him, Luther turned his head south and started the trudge to Tim and Alfred's house on Washington Street. When he passed the H&H Seafood House before approaching the bridge over the waterway to the inner harbor and before turning east on Texas Avenue, the vision of his mother, Sally, rose into his brain as it always did when he passed where she'd been a waitress for thirty years, and Luther smiled.

His mother had always been very good to him. When they'd told her Luther was different from other boys and needed to go to a special school, she'd shamed them into keeping him in the Cape May school and giving him extra help. It wasn't her fault the extra help hadn't been enough, and when everyone at the school sighed with relief the third time he didn't get into the eighth grade and Sally just pulled him out and set him to refinishing furniture at home, he'd stopped worrying about life. The kids at the school had made fun of him. He was always big and clumsy. He wasn't ugly or grotesque. Far from it. He was much too good looking and well built for his own good. Part of the sigh of relief at the school was that girls were noticing him— and a boy or two also—and were getting entirely too interested in the big-bodied, older boy in their classes.

He had developed quickly and it soon became apparent he had an attribute that could get very embarrassing at the school and that, although he would be a natural at football when—no, if—he got into middle school, it might not be the best idea if he was in locker room conditions with the other boys—and certainly not where any of the girls could see him.

Luther's name came from his father, who hadn't been around for more than a couple of days of Luther's life, having been not-too-gently convinced to leave town by dock workers in the harbor who were none too pleased with a big, strapping black man courting a white woman so intensely. He stayed around long enough for Sally to have gotten pregnant, however. You wouldn't have known that Luther had any black in him, though—unless you saw him undressed, which became a challenge for his schoolmates to accomplish. The one attribute that Luther inherited from his father was male equipment that was decidedly darker than the rest of him. And the ease with which Luther's father had gotten his way with Sally might have resulted from the size of his equipment, a trait that Luther also inherited.

It was upon this unusual attribute that many of the rumors about Luther as he grew older were based, although, despite the fears of many Cape May parents, as yet none of their daughters had come forth with news they didn't want to hear.

When Tim and Alfred had agreed to take Luther on at their Pink Poodle antiques store in a pink Victorian house in the tourist area on Decatur Street, more than one father had told them in no uncertain terms to keep a tight rein on the young man. The two store owners, who lived together in a white Victorian house in the less-touristy area of Washington Street, stepped up to the task.

Because he was big and a little clumsy, they had been reluctant to let Luther near their antique store. But they were careful to keep the lumbering giant away from their rooms filled with more delicate antiques. And in spite of the dangers of having him around, Luther had learned well the craft of furniture refinishing, so they put him to work in the workshop behind their house and in the storerooms at the antique store.

* * * *

"Luther, Luther, Lumbering Luther."

The taunting litany started as soon as Luther turned onto Texas Street. He was only four blocks from home, though, so he tucked his chin in, set a slight scowl on his face, and kept walking.

"How ya hangin', Luther? Show us how you're hangin'," the taunting continued.

There were four of them, young guys walking back toward the town from the technical college that was located near where Ocean Avenue split off from Lafayette. They had attended the elementary school where Luther had been a student for a couple of years longer than the standard and still hadn't moved up, but they weren't the brightest bulbs in the chandelier either. He'd failed to get into the eighth grade, but they had barely managed to get out of the twelfth.

There were actually five of them, but the fifth young man was hanging back. He'd been walking several paces behind the other four anyway, but when they started taunting Luther, he stopped in his tracks and just watched.

One of the youths picked up a rock from the side of the road. And then another one did. Looking at each other, wanting the other youth to initiate that attack, they both went into a grin. "One, two, three."

Only one of the rocks hit Luther, but it hit him in the chest as he turned to see what they were doing, and it was sharp-edged, tearing his shirt and making blood start to seep across his white shirt front.

"Hey, watch out," the fifth youth called out. "There's a police car coming."

The four taunters evaporated, and Luther swiveled his head, looking for the police car. He liked watching the police cars cruising around. He preferred watching fire trucks, but they didn't cruise around much.

"I don't see no police car," he called out, his voice full of disappointment.

"There isn't one. I just wanted the guys to stop throwing rocks at you." The young man was approaching Luther. He put his hand on the giant's arm when he reached him. "You look like you're hurt."

"I go home now anyway. I have bandages. I have a real first aid kit in the workshop." Luther was beaming like someone had just given him a hospital.

"I'll come with you and make sure it gets bandaged properly . . . if that's OK with you. It will be a little difficult for you to bandage your own chest, I think."

"Well, OK. Tim and Alfred don't like me to have people at the house. But OK, I think."

"My name's Keith," the young man said, as they turned and branched off south onto Washington Street from Texas.

"My name's Luther."

"I know," Keith said. "I've wanted to meet you."

When they got to Tim and Alfred's house, Luther guided Keith around to a building in back. He looked around to see if anyone was watching. With the rhythm of each step on the way to the house, Luther's mind was repeating "No visitors," the litany that Tim and Alfred had drummed into him for months when he'd first come there. He was afraid that someone might see Keith and him and tell Tim or Alfred—especially Alfred, who got angry so easily—that he'd let someone in the workshop without their permission.

From the kitchen window of the house just to the north of Tim and Alfred's house, old Mrs. Watson watched the two young men going to the building at the back of the house and took note of Luther looking furtively around. She pursed her lips and shook her head. She had been very displeased when she'd heard those two men—she always thought of them as "those two men" with a little sneer when she said the word "men"—were bringing the young man to live with them. She'd known there would be no good coming from that. And now that retard was bringing young men home himself. Well, she thought, at least it wasn't young women. That would really be something nobody would want.

* * * *

"There, it's not too bad. But I don't think you could have wound this bandage around your chest very well yourself."

"Thanks . . . Keith," Luther answered in a half whisper. Keith had been standing very close to him and had moved his hands on Luther's well-muscled chest perhaps a bit more than was required to clean and bandage the wound. Keith remained close in, standing between Luther's beefy thighs, as Luther perched on the stool in the kitchen-dining-living room area, with a double bedstead peeking around the corner of the L-shaped room attached at the rear of the workshop. Luther had been reluctant to let Keith in this room; he'd wanted to have the dressing done in the workshop on the driveway side of the building, but Keith had insisted that it was too dusty in there to treat a wound.

"Luther."

"Yes, Keith?"

"Those other guys. What they were saying to you?"

"I didn't listen to them. My mother told me not to listen to words like that."

"They wanted you to show it."

After a brief pause, with Luther looking sheepish. "Yeah, I guess."

"We're friends now, aren't we Luther?"

"Yeah, sure."

"Friends show. Could I see it, Luther? I wouldn't tell anyone."

Luther was quiet for a couple of moments. Keith had his hands cupping Luther's bulging biceps.

"Please, Luther. We're friends, right?"

"Yeah, right. Well, OK, I guess."

Luther reached down and unzipped the fly of his trousers. A thick snake of a dark brown cock rolled out of the recess. It approached a foot in length and was fat in thickness. And it was half hard.

Luther was blushing. "I'm sorry. It sometimes—"

"Can I hold it, Luther? It's a very nice one."

"Well, I guess . . . uh, that feels—"

"It's OK, Luther. We're friends. I just want to see how big it can get." Keith was holding it in two hands that didn't overlap and was slowing stroking it. "It's black, Luther. Very different."

"Uh, brown."

"Yes, but almost black. You shouldn't keep it secret. You should share it."

"Well, I—"

"Will you share it with me, Luther? We're friends. Would you put it inside me?"

"I don't know about that. Tim and Alfred tells me I can't have anyone in here. Maybe you'd better—"

"Well, no, not in here, of course. Tim and Alfred are absolutely right about that. But there's a place where it's OK. They just didn't have a chance to tell you that part."

"There's a place it's all right here?"

"Yes. In the workshop. There's a nice low table in the workshop, Luther. I saw it when we came in. And when I saw it, I thought to myself, Keith, there's a very nice fuck fuck table."

Luther looked a little dubious, but he was breathing heavily from the stroking Keith had continued giving his cock.

"I bet you didn't even know you had a fuck fuck table, Luther. They are pretty rare. I guess Tim and Alfred have one because they run an antique store. They probably couldn't turn down buying it when they found one. That's where it's perfectly all right for you to put this inside me. Will you take me to your table, Luther?"

"Well, I don't know."

"Please, Luther. Friends are . . . you know . . . friendly to each other."

* * * *

"Oh gawd, oh holy shit. Yes, Luther. More. Push harder."

Keith was laying on his back on the surface of the low table in the workshop, his legs open to Luther, who was standing between his thighs, hunched over him, with his fists pushing into the table on either side of Keith's quaking shoulders.

He was grunting and groaning, trying to get it all inside Keith's ass. One of Keith's hands was encasing the root of Luther's cock, trying to take it all inside himself as his beleaguered channel slowly expanded to accommodate the huge staff. Keith moved his hands to palming Luther's bulbous buttocks and pulling Luther as close into his trembling ass as possible.

Keith had had nothing like this before. He'd taken cock from the best in the technical school. But he'd never had it anything like this before. The rumors had gone around about Luther and the monster cock and that it was black. Keith had trembled at the thought of that inside him—and he doubted that it really was black. But it was close enough—and bigger than anything he'd ever seen before, let alone serviced. His channel was slowly giving way, trembling at the feel of the pulsating veins running down the cock and fully aware of the bulbous head on the monster phallus as it dug ever deeper inside him. It was a ebony beauty, and it was pulsing inside him. What he hadn't been able to come even close to getting inside his mouth was deep inside his channel.

Keith went up on his elbows and searched for Luther's lips with his. Luther looked surprised, but he took the kiss and started to hum happily.

"All of it. Give me all of it, Luther," Keith cried out as he arched his back and threw his head back. He locked his legs at the small of Luther's back and dug his fingers into Luther's hips.

He panted and gave a little surprised scream as Luther thrust harder inside him, and Keith felt his channel walls expanding, his muscles there shimmering over the invading staff, images of a baseball bat floating before his eyes. Just like "Shoeless" Joe Jackson's Black Betsy bat.

Luther grunted. "It's OK? You said you wanted—"

"Oh gawd yes," Keith cried. "It's in. We did it. Oh shit, we—" He was about to tell Luther what to do next, but Luther had figured that out all by himself. "Oh shit yessss!"

Keith sucked in his breath as he felt the huge dick pulling back out, slowly, a good eight or nine inches. Then, "Oh holy christ!" as it slid back in all the way. Back and in. Back and in. Backandin, backandin. BACKANDIN.

"Oh shit! fuck me, fuck me, fuckmefuckme! I'm gonna come. Oh, God." Whimpering as, after he had come, Luther kept on fucking.

* * * *

19

"Tim told me you would be here, Luther."

"Oh, hello, Mr. Sims. You surprised me. I'm washing Alfred's car."

"Yes, you are, and you're doing a very fine job of it too."

Grant Sims hadn't really asked Tim or Alfred if he could come over to the Washington Street house. But he'd wanted to come. He'd wanted to come for some time. He'd even pulled some old chairs and a drop-leaf table out of his attic and took them to Tim and Alfred for refinishing because he'd wanted to visit Luther here.

Mr. Sims was a physical education teacher at the school where Luther had spent three years trying to get into the eighth grade. Mr. Sims had done what he could to keep Luther in the gym program there if for no other reason than to be around when the boys took their showers. It had been a sad day for him when he was told that Luther wouldn't be coming back for a fourth crack at advancement—and another naked shower in the school's locker room.

He was in ninth heaven that he'd found Luther washing Alfred's vintage Thunderbird in the driveway of the white Victorian house on Washington Street, after having checked and made sure that both Tim and Alfred were at their antique store. Quite unconsciously Luther was wearing nothing but gym shorts. Gym shorts he'd gotten soaked while working on Alfred's car and that were pulled low on his hips by the water logging. The shorts were so plastered to his body that nothing was left to the imagination—especially since, with drawn breath, Mr. Sims was quite sure he could see something brown and smooth and knobby peeking out of one of the leg holes of Luther's gym shorts.

But that didn't seem to either be something that concerned Luther or made him the least bit self-conscious. Even if he caught glimpses of the disapproving scowl of Mrs. Watson in her kitchen window, he didn't seem a bit affected by the magnificence of his muscled body—or that he hung so low inside his water-soaked shorts—or that the blackness of his cock, clearly discernible in his soaked shorts, was a shocking attention getter.

"Uh. I thought I'd check on that furniture you're refinishing for me," Mr. Sims said. "Tim told me you had it here at the house. In the workshop."

"Yeah, I do," Luther said, as he continued to rinse the soap off the Thunderbird.

"Well, could I see it?"

"I don't know. Tim and Alfred always say—"

"That's what I came over to see, Luther. Tim said it was here in the workshop. He wants me to see the furniture. Have you done any work on it?"

This was the most dangerous moment for Grant. What if the answer was no? How would he maneuver Luther into the double bed in the studio apartment behind the workshop if there hadn't been any work on the furniture yet?

21

"Yeah, I've worked on one of the chairs. It didn't need much refinishing. All three pieces are in pretty good shape."

"So, can we go in and look at it?"

"OK, I guess. If Tim says it's OK."

Grant didn't respond to that. Tim didn't even know he was here.

Luther stood there, water streaming out of the end of the hose and onto the trunk of the Thunderbird.

"Maybe you should turn the hose off and show me into the workshop," Grant said. He said it very quietly, trying to sound calm. Didn't this lunkhead get it? And, god, speaking of hose. Gotta get some of that. I've been salivating for that for years.

"OK." Luther smiled and went over and turned off the hose. "The workshop is back here," he said as he moved toward the end of the driveway.

I fuckin' know where the friggin' workshop is, Grant screamed in his mind. But what he said was. "Good, so let's go there."

If he'd looked around like Luther had done when he brought Keith to the building in the rear of the lot, he'd probably have seen the curtains in Mrs. Watson's kitchen shaking with indignation. But neither he nor Luther looked.

"This is it," Luther said when they entered the dimly lit workshop. "Want me to turn on a light?"

22

"No, that's not necessary," Grant answered. He was glad that Luther had pointed the chair out. He could tell that some work had been done on it, but the furniture hadn't really needed to be refinished. It would have been hard for him to tell that chair from the one that hadn't been touched yet.

He took his time looking over the chair, spending the time trying to figure out his next move.

Luther was wandering aimlessly around the workshop. He'd picked an old, rusted harmonica off the shelf of a bookcase and was trying to get a tune out of it without much success. The tune sounded as rusty as the harmonica looked.

"You've got some really interesting furniture in here," Grant Sims said, reaching for anything to start up a conversation that could be bent to his purposes.

"We sure do. Some of it is real rare," Luther answered, with a sloppy smile on his face. "You ever seen a fuck fuck table?" he casually asked as he brushed by the table where he'd thoroughly fucked his new friend, Keith. Keith had been back twice for fuck sessions.

"Excuse me? A what?" Grant looked up in shock, not believing what he'd heard.

"A fuck fuck table. Lower than a dining table. My friend told me this was good for fucking. He said it was a fuck fuck table. And he said Tim and Alfred put it in here because this was where I should fuck fuck. They told me not to bring anyone into my room. But my friend said they put this fuck fuck table in here just for me."

Still somewhat bewildered, Grant responded in a croaking voice, "Yes, it's a very nice fuck fuck table, Luther. I like using those too. I would like to be your fuck fuck friend too. I see that you need a new harmonica. I have a nice new shiny one. Would you like to have it? I would like to give it to you as a present—if, of course, you have a present for me."

* * * *

"Yes, yes. Give it to me. GIVE IT TO ME. GIVEITTOME! Ram it in!" Grant Sims screamed when Luther did just that, as Grant stood on the floor and bent over Luther's fuck fuck table, grasping the opposite rim of the table with white-knuckled fists, pounding his cheek on the surface of the table, and letting the tears flow.

Luther, humming and thinking of the new harmonica he would have, stood between Grant's spread thighs from the rear, held his old gym teacher's waist with his hands, and pounded the older man's ass hard and deep. Mr. Sims had asked for it hard, Mr. Sims had been Luther's gym teacher, and Luther always wanted to please his teachers.

It was bigger, thicker, blacker even than Sims had remembered from four years earlier. And, oh gawd, it was splitting him. And he'd taken it all. The glory of the biggest, blackest cock he'd ever had.

"Oh, please, yesss!"

Luther was pushing him up on the surface of the table, and following him up. Sims was raised on his knees, his chest and cheek flat on the table top, his fists still gripping the opposite rim. Yodeling for it. Luther was crouched over his hips and fucking him like a dog.

Just like Grant Sims had fantasized for the past four years. Who would have known it would be this easy?

Afterward, Grant stopped Luther as they reached the door to the driveway.

"Tim might not like me giving you a new harmonica. So, we'll just keep me being here a secret, shall we? I'll be back in a few days with your new harmonica."

"And will you want to use the fuck fuck table again?" Luther was giving his former gym teacher a friendly, open smile. Not the least bit of embarrassment or concern. Just like what they had just been doing was the natural thing to do. His friend, Keith, had told him it was the natural thing for young men their ages to do—that all young men did this at this age. Luther wanted to show that he was as good as any other young man his age. He wanted to do what they all were doing. He was happy that his new friend, Keith, had told him about this. It was fun. But then there were a few things that even Keith didn't know.

25

"Oh, yes, Luther. I very much will want to use the fuck fuck table again. If it wasn't about time for Tim and Alfred to come home, I'd want to use it again right now." Grant felt brave saying that. He felt so reamed out that he wouldn't be able to put his legs together for a week. But he'd taken it. It was a telephone pole, and he'd had it all inside him. And he could hardly wait until he'd recovered enough to ride it again.

"We can't go into my room, you know," Luther said, all innocent smile. "Tim and Alfred say I can't bring friends into that room."

"That's why they put your fuck fuck table out here in the shop, I'm sure," Grant said. "They want you to fuck fuck out here. And this is fine with me."

You don't know just how fine, Grant was thinking. You might be retarded, but you do the best cocking in the State of New Jersey. And you don't even know it. Huge and black and a power driver. Oh, gawd.

Luther just smiled and waved as Grant Sims walked bowlegged to the car he'd parked on the street. The kitchen window curtains in Mrs. Watson's house ruffled angrily.

CHAPTER TWO: TAKING CARE OF BUSINESS

"Can you let me see it?" Father Paul asked. "My, my, what a very nice, big one."

Luther stood shyly at the church door at the end of mass while Father Paul took the picture the young man had been drawing during his homily from his hand and examined it with an interest that didn't seem too feigned. Luther had trouble sitting through the church service. He always had. Since his mother brought him here as a child, she'd given him one of the children's activity packets the church provided to hold his attention through the mass. Working with that while the service went on around him always kept him quiet and content. He'd gotten older, but he hadn't stopped entertaining himself with the packets.

"A secretary desk. And drawn with such precision," Father Paul said. "I can see that you are making good use of your training in furniture design."

This was said with some genuine admiration. Father Paul was, indeed, impressed with Luther's drawing talent. Luther stood before him, the two still in a handshake, while the line of parishioners waiting to greet and rush home to their lunches built up behind them. Thank God this child of limited means has found a true talent provided by thee, the priest intoned in his mind.

And then in added prayer in his thoughts that he hoped God was too busy to hear, Father Paul also said a little prayer of thanks that Luther had been too dim to fully understand some liberties the priest had taken with him earlier in life. Well, somewhat more than "some," he admitted to himself.

"But the tall brown tower next to the desk. I don't quite understand how that fits in."

"Umm, don't know father. I dream some when I draw. I don't know what I was thinking."

"That's fine, Luther. But it looks so out of place with that nicely drawn desk. Why don't you take some scissors when you get home and divide the drawings—and if you didn't want the tower one, you could give it to me and I will throw it away for you."

The priest knew full well what Luther had drawn in his daydreaming and what its reference point was. And it was making him feel hot and was stirring both memories and something more physically demanding in his body. It was a time to be glad that priests wore robes.

Giving Luther an affectionate pat on the shoulder, he propelled the young man on down the church steps and turned to the next parishioner in line and widened his smile. He was worried about Luther and what was in his future—and, perhaps, a bit, what he might someday say about his past. But Father Paul would think more on that later.

Luther gave a little smile of his own and started out across the church's lawn for the walk home. He might divide the picture, but he liked both. He'd keep them both.

When he looked up, he saw that Mrs. Sims was standing on the walk and looking at him. She seemed to be waiting for him. She was the Mrs. Sims of the Mr. Sims, who had been Luther's gym teacher and who now was one of his special friends. Luther liked Mrs. Sims better than he liked Mr. Sims, although he liked both just fine. She had been his teacher too. She had been his English teacher and she had spent extra time with him without being asked and had always been especially nice to him. She was in church alone, without Mr. Sims, today. That wasn't unusual. Mr. Sims always said he'd rather stay home and open his veins with a butter knife then walk into a church—and their wedding day may have been the last time he'd done so—walked into a church, that is.

As Luther approached Mrs. Sims, something in the back of his brain told him he should be apprehensive about something, but he couldn't grasp what that might be. She was giving him a big smile, so he knew it couldn't be anything very serious.

"There you are, Luther. I've been waiting to talk to you. I see that you were showing Father Paul a picture you drew in church. May I see it, please?"

"Sure." Luther handed the drawing to her.

"This is a very, very nice, drawing, Luther," Mrs. Sims said after inspecting it. There was a little catch in her voice when she said it, though. And Luther didn't notice that she didn't look into his face when she said that. He blushed in appreciation and whispered a "Thank you." He didn't notice that she looked a bit flushed too.

"It's so nice that I'd like to have it, if you are giving it away," she said.

"Well, sure, if you want it." Luther hadn't been planning to give it away. He had meant to try crafting that secretary. But the image of the design was in his mind—he was good at holding images in his brain. He guessed he could draw that again without any problem. Maybe that would be what he'd do right now when he got home.

"What I stopped you for, though, Luther, is that, if you'd like to earn a little extra money, I have some heavy-lifting, and reaching-up jobs in the house I need some young, strapping man like you to do for me. Do you think you'd be interested?"

"Yeah, sure," Luther answered. Mrs. Sims had always been very nice to him. He didn't mind one bit being nice back. And he wasn't paying full attention to her anyway. He was changing some trim work on the secretary in his mind.

"Some day this week between 3:30 and 5:00 in the afternoon, maybe? I'll be home from school and Mr. Sims will still be at intramural practice. He doesn't like for there to be fussing around in the house while he's there."

"Yeah, sure," Luther answered.

"You'll remember now, won't you?"

"Yeah, sure."

"So, you'll come by when?"

"Sometime this week."

"Between what times?"

"Ummm."

"Between 3:30 and 5:00. In the afternoon. Can you repeat that for me?"

"Yeah sure. Between 3:30 and, ummm—"

"And 5:00." Mrs. Sims repeated patiently. "In the afternoon." She'd always been patient with Luther. That's why he liked her so much.

"And 5:00," he said. "Yeah, sure. I'll come. Now I gotta go to the store. Tim and Alfred, they want me at the store this afternoon. I gotta go help them."

Luther was beaming so wide at remembering just now that he was headed to the store rather than home and at the prospect of being needed to help at the store that Mrs. Sims nearly teared up. What are we going to do with you, you dear, dear, manchild? Mrs. Sims thought, as she watched Luther turn and start humming as he walked toward Decatur Street, near the beach. She looked at the picture Luther had drawn again, folded it, put it in her purse, and snapped the clasp of the purse tightly shut.

* * * *

It wasn't exactly a crash, but it had the effect of bringing both Tim and Alfred posthaste into the room.

"What the hell?" Alfred exclaimed. "What are you doing in this room, Luther?"

Alfred was the little, frenetic one, always bouncing around and nervous about this and that. He also was the one who knew what to buy from an estate sale and for how much—and had a very good idea who he could unload it on at twice the price.

"You told me to turn the lamps on so the customers would see the lights on. I did that in the dining table room. And

32

then that room was all lit up and this one was too dark and so I . .
."

"Didn't I tell you never, ever to come into the crystal room?" Alfred exclaimed. Nearly every time Alfred opened his mouth, he was exclaiming.

"Now don't fret, dear," the just-arrived Tim said. He was the hippy one, the tall, thin one, with the long hair he kept tied back in a pony tail but down on his shoulders at home. The one who moved like he was a dancer and who fluttered with his hands. He also was the one who kept the Pink Poodle afloat with his accounting abilities and his skill with reining Alfred in on the grandiose schemes and monster purchases.

"No harm was done, was it Luther?" Tim continued "That's the lamp we heard, wasn't it? It isn't broken. The shade's just a little bent. You can set it back up now."

"I told you never—" Alfred was still fuming. It caused Luther's hand to start to shake. He didn't like being yelled out. And just for doing what he'd been told to do. He'd been told to turn the lamps on. This lamp wasn't turned on. He was just doing what he'd been told to do.

"Shush, baby, you're going to make him drop it again. It's OK, Luther, set the lamp up. Yes, like that. Now there are some boxes in the attic, by the stairs. Could you bring them down to the workroom here, please? And do be careful with them. There's some chinaware in the boxes."

When Luther got to the workroom with the boxes, Tim was waiting for him. "Thank you, Luther. Place that on this table—gently please. And thank you for your help today. You can go on home now."

"But I only got—"

"That's fine, my boy. You've helped a lot and there's really nothing else we need you to do at the shop today. You can go home and work on that table you like."

"You mean it? You like me working on that table?"

"But, of course. Run along now. You're on your own for dinner tonight. Alfred and I have dinner and a play to go to."

As Luther was leaving by the side entrance, Tim and Alfred were talking in the front hall. He wasn't really listening to them, though.

"What are we going to do?" Alfred was grousing. "He'll smash all of our profit. Why do we keep him on?"

"Shush, shush, baby. He hasn't broken much—really, not much—yet. And you know why we keep him on."

Luther also was grousing a bit as he walked over to Ocean Street and then up to Washington for the long walk home. He was mumbling to himself about schedules and having working at the store done for this afternoon. He'd only turned on the lamps in two rooms. There were four other rooms. He'd been told to turn the lamps on. Tim had told him to turn the lamps on and Luther didn't want Tim thinking he didn't do a good job of what he was asked to do.

Luther didn't like disruptions in his schedule—except if something came up that was fun. That made him think about what Tim had said about the table just now. Tim had said it was fine for him to work out on the fuck fuck table. Luther had been finding that the fuck fuck had been making his body stronger. And it sure was fun. And Tim had said it was fine to do.

He heard the hail, "Hey there, Luther," and looked up and smiled.

Keith was walking in his direction, down Ocean toward the beach. He was wearing a Speedo and flip-flops and had on a white terry-cloth jacket with a big red cross on it.

"Hi, yourself, Keith." Luther smiled broadly, because every time he saw Keith he thought of fuck fuck friends. And Keith really looked good.

"Where you goin' on a Sunday afternoon, sport?"

Luther liked the names Keith called him. They weren't like the names the other guys called him. They were friendly and sometimes they made him feel funny below. Like when they were alone and Keith called him "Stud" or "Horse" or even "Monster" or "Black Superdaddy." Luther wasn't sure of those names at first, but he liked to hear them once Keith had told him what he meant by those.

"Home," Luther said somewhat petulantly. "They don't need me at the store this afternoon. So, I'm going home. Don't know what I'll do there, though. I was going to work at the store all afternoon."

"You could come with me. I'm on duty this evening over at Cape May Point beach. But I came down here early just to horse around on the main beach. I'm a lifeguard. Didn't I tell you that? It helps with the school bills."

"Horse around?" Luther asked, his brown knitted. "You mean fuck fuck with you on the beach?" Luther had just been thinking of one of the names Keith used for him when they were fucking.

"Sometime, yes," he said, with a laugh. "But not today." But then his face turned into a broad grin. "Yes, fucking this afternoon is a great idea, Luther. You want me to come home with you and climb up on the table?"

* * * *

"Oh, FUCKKK!" Keith was crying out. They were both on the fuck fuck table, Luther sitting back on his heels, his knees up under Keith's belly, with Keith's ass high on his lap and Keith's toes dug into the table top on either side and behind Luther's hips. Luther's monster cock was fully encased. He had Keith's wrists trapped in his fists; Keith's torso was arched back like an archery bow, and he was crying out his pleasure to the ceiling of the work room, as Luther rocked his channel back and forth on the deeply buried cock. "You're a stud. Give it to me. Faster on your Black Superdaddy club. Oh yes, fuck me!"

"Luther? Luther? You here, guy? Tim told me you'd be here."

Upon hearing the voice call him from the driveway, Luther released Keith's wrists and Keith fell forward and moaned deeply.

"That's Mr. Sims. He's here to give me a new harmonica," Luther said. "You'll have to hide. He wants to fuck fuck. Tim said it's OK, but I don't know about two."

"It's OK," Keith said wearily. "I'll hide. I know where." And then, while Luther was headed toward the door, Keith muttered, "For christ sake, at least put on your shorts."

Luther blushed and reached down for his shorts. Keith laughed, gathered up his clothes, and, when Luther turned to go to the door, he slipped through the back door and into Luther's room.

"It's a nice harmonica. Thanks, Mr. Sims. You want to see the chairs? I'm working on the second one now."

"Yes, please, Luther." And as he looked over the chair, he murmured, "Very nice, Luther. But you know I came for more than the chairs, don't you?"

"Yes, Mr. Sims." Luther looked down at the floor shyly. He was standing next to the fuck fuck table and he let his knuckles rub on the surface. He was glad that Tim had let him know it was OK to use the table. He'd been a little worried about that, even with what his friend, Keith, had told him.

"Gawd, Luther, it looks like you're hard. Look at how it's sticking out. Are you hard for me, son?"

"Maybe," Luther whispered. He thought it would be a bit too complicated to explain the hiding Keith, wherever he was hiding.

"Shit, I can't wait. Hard for me. Hop up on the table, son."

Luther sat up on the side of the fuck fuck table. Mr. Sims slipped off his T-shirt and shorts and briefs on his way to slipping Luther's shorts off, gasping at the size of the cock that came out of them, and spreading the young man's legs and coming in close between them. He grasped both his and Luther's cocks together, but he couldn't get his hand all the way around them. He began to gently stroke them together.

"Anyone ever done this with you before?" he asked. He didn't give Luther a chance to answer, though, as his other hand had pulled around to the back of Luther's neck and brought their faces together in a kiss.

Luther wasn't sure about the kissing, but it felt sort of good, and Mr. Sims seemed to be liking it.

After the kiss, Sims was hunched over him, still stroking their cocks together. Luther was staring at the man's nipples. They were large and puffed up.

"You want me to suck your tits, Mr. Sims? My friend . . ." Opps, he'd almost given a name. He didn't know if Keith would like that ". . . my friend likes me to suck his tits. He has a silver ring in one. That's my favorite—my favorite of his tits. He's got two, just like me . . . and just like you too."

"Yes, Luther," Sims said, in a hoarse voice, "I'd like you to suck my tits. Then I'll suck yours."

Sims licked his way down Luther's torso and Luther gave a little lurch and a moan as Sims's mouth came down over his cock.

The older man looked up. He was smiling. He placed the palm of a hand on Luther's chest and pressed. "Lay back now, Luther. I'll bet no one has given you head. Not this good."

Then he proceeded to do so. Luther had, in fact been given head before. Very nice head. But Mr. Sims hadn't actually put it in the form of a question, so Luther didn't answer. He did moan and groan, though, because this was very nice head indeed.

"Oh, gawd, you are such a horse. Oh, fuck, I gotta get this inside me."

That's what Keith had said, Luther thought, that he was a horse. So, maybe he really was a horse. Maybe he could canter home from the antique shop tomorrow. He almost chuckled out loud at his own joke. But he was thinking something else now.

Waves and waves of pleasure were flowing over him and he felt pressure inside.

"Uh, Mr. Sims. I think I got some of that white pee pee comin'. Maybe you don't want to get wet."

"No, you can't come yet," Sims said in a thick voice. "Here, we lay here, not moving, for a couple of minutes. Let me know when the feeling is gone. Then, do you remember when I had you and the other guys do pushups back at school?"

"Yeah. That was sort of fun. I could do a lot more than anyone else."

"You sure could. You think you still could do a hundred of them?"

"Yeah, sure."

* * * *

"Thirty-eight, thirty-nine, forty." Luther was gleefully keeping count.

Sims was on his belly on the fuck fuck table, stretched out, his rump slightly elevated to give Luther a good angle for deep stroking. Luther was doing pushups on top of him, the heel of his hands next to Sims's shoulders, his toes pressed into the table top just outside Sims's pulled-in ankles. Sims was getting it big in a constricted channel, and he was groaning and moaning the heavenly stuffing he was getting.

"Forty-one. You OK, Mr. Sims? Forty-twoandthree," Luther murmured with a bit of concern. "I'm . . . forty-five . . . not hurting you, am I? Forty-sixsevenand eight."

"Yes, I'm OK," Sims answered between groans. "Yes, you're hurting me. You're hurting me to heaven. Oh shit, it hurts good."

When Mr. Sims left, talking about that nice tin whistle he had to bring to Luther the next time, Luther remembered—if a bit belatedly—to look around the workshop for where Keith was hiding. He probably had gotten bored and left, Luther thought. He picked up his shorts and T and headed for the door to his room.

"Keith!" he said when he entered the room and saw Keith, still naked, legs spread, dick in his hand, and laying on his back in Luther's bed. "You know—"

"Oh, the fuck fuck table is just where you are supposed to start making friends, Luther. I'm sure Tim told you that. Maybe you just don't remember? Special friends can come in here."

"Well, I don't know."

"You got me all hot and bothered, Luther. You invited me here for fuck fuck. And then that other guy came along. I have waited patiently. What kind of host are you going to be for a special friend?"

* * * *

"Oh, jessssus, ride me, Stud!"

Luther had his knees up under the small of Keith's back this time, with Keith's ankles locked behind Luther's neck and his hands running through the hair on the back of Luther's head, holding Luther's mouth to his nipples.

Luther was releasing the suck frequently to cry out a gleeful "Bounce, bounce, squeak."

He was mimicking the sounds of the rocking bed as it creaked and groaned and squeaked its own objections and moved across the floor under the strength of the power driving Keith had begged for.

"Me too, me too," Keith panted as he was flung around like a rag doll between Luther's pounding cock and the rocking, giving bed.

"I'm gonna do it. Here it . . .!"

". . . Comes!" Keith cried out. "Me too. Fuckkk!"

They lay there, cooling down, holding in place except for Luther's licking and sucking lips on Keith's nipples.

"Nice," Luther murmured. "I like the one with the silver ring the best."

"You like rings?"

"Yeah. They make me feel funny. Good funny."

"Yes, I can feel that. You want to fuck me again, don't you? You get hard again fast."

"I'm sorry, Keith," Luther whispered.

"Oh, shit, don't be sorry. It's what I want too. And you know what else would be nice?"

"No, what?"

"You could have a ring too. A big one. And not in the nipple. In the head of your cock. You would be the best then. A barbarian."

"The best? A barbarian would be good?"

"The best. It arouses—turns you on—doesn't it? The thought of a big ole metal ring in your cock head. Punishing men deep inside with that. Making them moan for it. I can feel that you'd like that."

"Keith. Sorry, I need . . ."

"See that chair over there, Luther? I want you to dog fuck me on that chair."

* * * *

Rob could tell by the way Madge set the casserole dish down on the dining room table—hard—that she was still ticked. The two girls looked up, startled, and then gave each other a secret look and went back to buttering their rolls.

"You know the best fishing is at night, Madge. I only go out every other week. It puts food on the table."

"That's not the issue, now is it?" Madge said. She turned to the sink, jerked on the cold water, and then had to step back and turn it down to escape the backsplash.

"I've taken Luther out with me before. Two men can bring in more than double what one man can. I think you're being just a bit ridiculous."

"What would just a bit ridiculous look like, Rob? Would it be, oh, twice as good as a teeny ridiculous?" She had rounded on him. She was brandishing a long wooden spoon that made the girls scrunch down in their seats.

"I'm not going to be any part of driving a young man out of the town he was born in just because he was a bit slow," Rob muttered.

"There's that 'bit' word again. I'll tell you, Rob, there's been talk. Very soon now there's going to be more than talk. He's going to assault some young girl, and then you'll be sorry you coddled him—that you are willing to be associated with him."

"He'll do no such thing, Madge. Who's been telling you these stories? There's not a violent bone in that young man's body. He'd give you the shirt off his back—"

"Not in my sight, he won't."

"Is that what this is about? The rumors about how sexy—?"

"Rob Leighton, you shush." Madge inclined her head and pointed her spoon at the girls—who quite suddenly weren't so scrunched down in their chairs, eyes wide.

"There's nothing wrong with Luther, Madge. He's slow, but he's got a great, giving nature. I need someone to help me on an overnight fishing trip, and he needs people to treat him like he isn't some sort of freak."

"Well, I've heard that in some ways—"

"And if that were true, the best place for him to be would be out on the Atlantic on a fishing boat, now wouldn't it?"

"I just—"

"I don't want to hear any more about witch hunts, Madge. I wasn't even sure I'd go out to fish on Tuesday night. But now you can be sure I will—and that I'll take Luther with me if he wants to go. Case closed. Girls, spoon up some of the stuff in the casserole dish and eat it before it gets cold."

"Rob!" Madge exclaimed.

"Daddy said 'stuff,'" Muriel said. "Daddy called Mommy's food 'stuff.'" Both girls put their hands to their mouths and giggled.

* * * *

"Pretty sleek, isn't she?"

45

"Yes, she sure is," Luther answered. He was standing at the edge of the parking lot at Cape May Harbor, bare chested and in worn blue jeans, with a slit at one of the knees, his bare feet in a pair of thin sandals. The cabin cruiser was gleaming white and long and had at least three decks to it as far as Luther could see, not counting the top sundeck where a raven-haired woman with the slightest of bikinis on was stretched out on a deck lounger.

The man standing next to Luther was maybe in his early fifties. His once-dark hair had grayed at the temple. He wasn't as tall as Luther and was slimmer, but he looked like he spent a good amount of his time in the gym. His face was handsome, although someone more worldly wise than Luther could have seen that it had had a lot of work done on it. He was nattily decked out in white trousers and a white polo shirt, white deck loafers without socks, and a white sweater reversed on his back, with the arms loosely tied across his chest. He had a gold medallion nestled in his chest hair, dangling on a gold chain around his neck; a diamond ring large enough to choke a horse; and a Rolex watch. His hands were manicured and the sunglasses wedged in his hair cost more than Luther made in a year.

All of this swept right past Luther, though. The man had talked to him in a friendly manner and smiled at him. He was being real friendly. That was enough for Luther to be friendly back.

"Her name is Pamela."

"Oh, that's a nice name."

"The ship is called Pamela too. And it's pretty sleek too, if I do say so."

"Oh, sorry, I didn't mean—"

"Oh, I know you didn't. I was just joking with you. My name is Jonathan. Jonathan Payne. That's my boat. My wife too, for that matter."

"Umm. That's nice. I'm—"

"You're Luther. Yes, I know. I've checked around."

"You've checked around?"

"How would you like to do some cruising in that yacht, Luther?"

"Cruising? Me?"

"Yes, you. We can make it worth your while. Say $200 for a day cruise. We could go out now and come back tonight."

"Now?" Luther asked. He would have been a real dummy not to notice that Jonathan had the palm of a hand on the small of his back.

"Yes, of course now. Let's say $300."

"Uh, that sounds nice, but I promised to meet a friend at sunset. Down on the beach."

"Oh, hell, $500 and we'll have you back in the morning." Obviously Jonathan didn't realize that Luther had little sense for money. He might have had much more success by telling Luther how fast the yacht could cruise and how its engine worked.

"I'd love to go out in that yacht. Maybe some other day," was what Luther answered.

"Yes, maybe some other day," Jonathan repeated. He didn't seem that upset he hadn't succeeded. But with people like him, there always was another day.

"But you'd be willing to go out with us someday?"

"I'd love it. I have a friend to meet at sunset, though."

"So you said. Well, anytime you have for cruising come on down. If we're here, we'll be happy to have you . . . to take you out."

"Thanks, Mr. Payne. I'd like that."

"It's Jonathan. And, Luther, we'd show you a really good time. A really good time."

Luther smiled like he understood what he was being told.

"Oh, here, you have a speck on your jeans. Let me . . ." Without further asking, he let his hand run down Luther's crotch. He drew in his breath deeply at discovering how far he had to slide the hand to run out of what he was checking.

"Uh, thanks. I gotta go now. Bye."

"Bye, Luther. Tell you what, you go out on a cruise with us and I'll give you $1,000."

"That's great, Mr. Payne. Maybe I'll see you around."

Jonathan stood, shaking his head, and moving his hand on his crotch as he watched Luther jauntily walk away toward the Cape May beaches.

As Luther passed the H&H restaurant just off the wharf, he saw that one of the dishwashers there where Luther's mother had worked was waving to him. It was Chuck. Luther liked Chuck and waved back to him. It was nice to see old friends like Chuck smiling and waving. Seeing him there made Luther remember his mother, and remembering her always made him smile.

* * * *

Keith was policing his section of the beach, taking stray beach chairs and lounges back up to the rental stands, and bustling around late-leaving bathers. The beach had officially closed a half hour earlier, but it would take some time for some of the people to accept that. Keith wouldn't get pushy for a while.

He looked out toward the ocean and skipped a breath or two when he saw Luther standing there, at the edge of the surf, looking back at the sunset over Cape May and the lights in the town start to flicker on. He was bare-chested and in a pair of worn jeans. He was giving a little shy smile that always turned Keith on and had his hands in his pockets in an "Oh golly, gee whiz" pose. And that little dopey smile of his—the young Tom Selleck smile, Keith always thought.

"You came," Keith said as he walked down the beach to where Luther stood.

"You're right. It's right pretty to watch the town at night from the beach," Luther said.

"That's not the angle I wanted you to see—and it's not late enough to get a real good view of the lights of the town. We'll have to wait for a bit. Come on over and sit on the beach by the lifeguard stand. After I've cleaned the beach area up a bit more, I'll come sit with you and we'll talk until the beach is clear of people. Then you'll see what I was talking about."

When Keith had finished his cleanup duties, they sat by the lifeguard stand, on a large beach towel. Keith brought out two more, which they wrapped around their shoulders—Keith was just in his Speedo—against the breeze flowing across the beach. As the beach became more deserted, the closer together they sat, until they were shoulder to shoulder, with both towels overlapping around them.

Keith put an arm around Luther's waist under the towels, and Luther did the same around Keith's shoulder. Keith reached over with a hand and unzipped Luther, fished his cock out, and started slow pumping it.

"Tell me, Luther. If you could be anywhere in the world and you didn't have to worry about money, where would you go?"

"I don't know," Luther answered. "Where would you go?"

"I'd go straight to Key West, Florida. I'd dance on a bar and let all of the studs there fuck me into eternity. So, come on, where would you go?"

"I'd go right here, I guess," Luther answered after several moments of thought.

"Here on the beach, with me giving you a hand job?"

"Uh, this is nice. But, no, here in Cape May. Day to day stuff."

"Oh, come on, that's not showing any imagination."

"I think I like it right here. I have a job and I'm learning to make things. And I have nice fuck fuck friends like you."

"You're serious, aren't you? I said you could have all the money you needed to live anywhere."

"I like what I have."

"OK, say you could be anyone you wanted to be. Who would that be?"

"Hmm. That's hard. I like me. I know I'm a little slow. But I get there. I get what I want."

"Do you now? Well, you know who I wish I could be?"

"No, who."

"You."

"Why?" Luther was truly surprised.

"Well, because you have a three-hand thick black monster snake that everyone wants inside them."

"Oh, go on, be serious. I don't got no snake. Alfred wouldn't let me have no pet in my room."

"OK, not completely serious. I'll settle for being the second most lucky man in the world."

51

"Who's that?"

"Me, of course. Because in ten minutes I'm going to have a three-hand thick black monster snake inside me."

Luther showed him a dubious expression.

"A snake. A cock. And not just any cock. A big, long one like this."

"You want me to fuck fuck you? Right here?"

"No. Out there—in the water. Off with those jeans and I'll race you into the ocean. It's time you saw what I invited you here to see."

"Out in the ocean?"

"Yes. Now." Keith jumped up, stripped off his Speedo, and raced out to the water. Luther, slower to react and longer to get his jeans off, stumbled along behind.

"Here. This is about right," Keith said when they got out just before the waves started to break and were in water that was about three-and-a-half feet deep. "Turn facing the town over my shoulder and put me on your cock."

Luther embraced Keith from behind and lifted him up. Keith reached in and, with a groan, impaled himself on Luther's cock.

"There, see the lights of Cape May?" Keith murmured between pants. "Isn't that something, seeing them from out here at night. Now, fuck me flying. I want a flying fuck. Just like this afternoon before that other guy came."

Luther took Keith's wrists and hunched down a bit in the water to counterbalance Keith arching his torso out toward the shore and away from Luther's groin. Keith locked his ankles under Luther's buttocks and began leveraging off his feet, with the aid of the water, and fucking himself in short, deep strokes on Luther's cock.

Faster and faster he pumped, crying out his need and his passion to the noise-swallowing waves breaking on the sand until he cried out in ejaculation. Luther turned Keith on his cock then, with Keith's arms around Luther's neck, his ankles locked once more below Luther's buttocks, and his mouth suckling on Luther's nipples, as, hands encasing Keith's waist, Luther moved Keith's channel up and down on his cock until he too ejaculated.

When they returned to the beach, Keith moved to pick up his Speedo, but Luther pushed him down on the towel beside the lifeguard stand on his back. He held Keith flat on his back with hands planted where Keith's arms met his chest. Luther covered Keith's cock with his mouth, proved that he could get that and Keith's balls in his mouth at the same time, and gave Keith a yodeling—Keith doing the yodeling—blow job.

Keith was whimpering when he came and telling Luther how good that was and that he'd never expected anything like that. Luther pushed Keith's legs apart and as Keith cried out, "Oh, Fuck!" Luther split his channel with his rehardened cock and did just that.

A male couple stealing along the beach toward their own tryst, stopped nearby, and one of them whispered, but loud enough for both Keith and Luther to hear them, "Gawd I wish I was being fucked like that—and with that."

"Maybe—" the other one attempted to say.

"Get off the damn beach. It's closed," Keith cried out. "And this is *my* stud horse cock!"

Later when they both were letting the sea breeze cool them down, Keith whispered. "To hell with Key West. I get what I want right here."

CHAPTER THREE: THE POWER AND AUDACITY OF MONEY

"When are you gonna fix breakfast?"

"When are you going to untie me and take your dick out of me?"

"Now you know that ain't gonna happen for a while," Zack said. "You can feel me hardening inside you. You know we're gonna fuck again. I was just tryin' to make a joke here."

"We have time for chocolate chip pancakes or a fuck, Zack," Cliff Trent answered, "And you're hurting me, making my body go numb, you big lug."

"Sorry 'bout that. You picked me because of how big I was. What I got swingin'. But what would you choose?"

Cliff gave Zack a withering look and a groan, and Zack then shrugged and took much of the weight of his body off Cliff. They were in their queen-sized bed in Cliff's apartment. Cliff was on his back with his wrists tied to the brass headboard above his head, and Zack was on top of him, deep inside Cliff, his cock recovering from their early-morning fuck. Zack moved his legs from on top of Cliff's and planted a knee on either side of Cliff's thighs. He lifted his chest and propped himself up on his elbows on either side of Cliff's chest. He pulled his pelvis back and rammed it forward, deep inside his partner's channel, snapping Cliff's head back and causing him to raise his own pelvis and grind the heels of his feet into the sheets.

"Oh, fuck!" he howled. Back and ram, back and ram.

"You. I'd choose the fuck!" Cliff cried out. He looked down the line of the mammoth, but ripped, chocolate-brown chest and flat belly to where he could see the root of the black cock assaulting his channel and the black balls slapping against this thighs. "Oh, yes, fuck me!"

Back and ram, back and ram. "Four. When I hit sixty, I want you to come," Zach said, with a laugh. "I'll shoot off at seventy. Then we'll have chocolate chip pancakes."

A half hour later, Cliff Trent stood behind the kitchen counter, in an apron and nothing else, and shoveled pancakes onto Zack's plate with a spatula.

"Hey, these don't have chocolate chips in them!"

Zack had showered and dressed in his brown sanitation worker uniform and his big construction boots. He was only working a half shift today. If he was working a full shift, he would have been out of here shortly after five and Cliff wouldn't have gotten the two morning fucks. But if Cliff hadn't gotten the two morning fucks, he wouldn't be standing in his kitchen shoveling pancakes and worrying about being late to his own job.

Zack would tie him up and fuck him again in the late afternoon after Cliff got home from his own job as a social worker. The chocolate monster's big dick was the reason Cliff kept him around. After their afternoon session and a dinner fixed by Cliff, Zack would be off for his night job as a bouncer at a club. When Zack got home from that, he'd wake Cliff up giving him his night fuck. This had been going on for three months. Cliff was getting worn out, but he was a happy worn out.

And this morning he had to get to work on time. Some old lady was coming in to complain about what some young neighbor of hers was doing. Cliff long ago had stopped thinking his job was either important or fulfilling. Zack was filling. That's what Cliff looked forward to these days.

"I didn't have time to look for chocolate chips," Cliff muttered. "You're lucky you got pancakes rather than warm toast. I haven't even had time to shower yet."

"But you like walking around with the swishy feeling of my cum inside you, don't cha?"

"Let's not be crude, Zack," Cliff said. But he didn't answer the question. Zack was a big-volume ejaculator—he did everything big—and, yes, Cliff did get a little thrill from walking around with Zack's cum inside him. "You eat that and stay out of

57

the way. I've got to shower and dress and go listen to an old busybody lady tattle on her neighbors."

"You'll be home by five, though?"

"Yes, I wouldn't miss it for the world."

"Good. I'll be waitin' for you."

I sure hope so, Cliff thought, but I don't know how much longer we can go on like this.

* * * *

Luther watched Cliff Trent climb the stairs to the front porch at the Pink Poodle. He was distinctive, because he looked like he was here on business other than buying antiques. His jaw was set tight. Alfred thought he was a disgruntled customer he couldn't quite place. Tim thought he was a process server. Luther thought he'd be nice looking—looking like a possible friend—if he wasn't frowning like that. And when he saw Luther, through the window, standing in the dining room furniture room, the man frowned more deeply and looked away.

Luther watched him march through the hallway and back toward the office where Tim kept the accounts.

Luther didn't have much time to think about him, though, because right behind him came that smart-looking man with the yacht, Jonathan, and his wife, Pamela. They were climbing the stairs too. And when they came in, they turned to the right and into the crystal room, although Jonathan did notice Luther standing in the room across the hall and gave him a smile and a wink and a little wave of his hand.

Luther gave a little wave back. Then he crossed the hallway and stood in the doorway to the crystal room.

"Hello," Jonathan said. "Your name is Luther, isn't it? You remember me from when we met in the marina, don't you?"

"Yes, sir."

"This is my wife, Pamela. This is Luther, dear. I told you about him."

"He's very nice," Pamela said. She had sunglasses on, though, so Luther wasn't really sure she was looking at him. He didn't notice then that she wasn't just looking at him; she was eating him up with her eyes. After getting an eye full, she moved into the crystal room.

"We're just looking around," Jonathan said. "You work here, do you?"

"Yes, sir. But I can't help you in that room. Tim and Alfred, they don't let me in that room."

"That's fine. We won't be long. In fact, we are on our way to lunch. Would you care to join us?—and we can talk about you taking that cruise on our yacht. We'll be leaving for Newport tomorrow afternoon. We could take the cruise today. But first lunch."

"I don't know if Tim and Alfred will let me go to lunch. Usually they go to lunch about now. And when I'm here, they leave me in charge. I sit out on the front porch and point to the 'gone to lunch' sign on the door while Tim and Alfred are gone. If anyone wants to come into the store, I point to the sign. They lock the door, but I sit out there on the porch and am in charge while they're gone."

"Well, perhaps they'll make an exception today. Shall we ask them?"

"I don' know," Luther said, his voice giving an edge of skepticism. "I'm supposed to work this afternoon." Anyone could see, though, that he'd like the adventure of someone taking him to lunch—especially a couple as well dressed as Jonathan and Pamela.

Just then Tim came out of his office and into the hall and called up the stairs for Alfred to come down. He seemed perturbed.

"Excuse me," Jonathan said, saddling up to Tim. "We're friends of Luther here and wondered if you'd mind if we took him to lunch today. We were thinking of the Pilot House Restaurant. It's just up the street on Carpenters Lane."

"Luther to lunch?" Tim said it like he was trying to confirm that someone had declared that aliens had landed in the middle of Decatur Street. He seemed to have stopped fully processing at the suggestion that this obviously wealthy couple might be friends of Luther's.

"And then after lunch, we could come back here and do some shopping," Jonathan added.

This obviously sealed the deal, as Tim said, "It's certainly all right with me if that's what Luther wants to do." And then he called up the staircase again, telling Alfred that he was needed in the office right away. His voice had sounded like he was relieved Luther was going off for lunch.

* * * *

"There, was that cheeseburger good, Luther?" Jonathan asked. They were sitting out on the covered verandah overlooking Carpenters Lane. Jonathan had tried to get Luther to order something more exotic—or at least more like an elegant beach resort meal—but Luther had wanted a cheeseburger. Jonathan had gone for the Tialapia Francaise and Pamela the Portabella Paninni. They'd split a bottle of Pino Grigio. Luther had a Coke.

"Yes, real good, thanks."

"Did you like what you heard about our Yacht?"

"Yeah sure. You have a fuck fuck table? They are nice, but they are hard to find. It would be good if you had one."

"Excuse me? A what?" Jonathan was shocked. Pamela just turned her head back to the men and gave a little amused smile.

"A table for fuck fuck. You want me to go out on the ocean with you to fuck fuck, don't you?"

"Excuse me?" Again from Jonathan.

"When we were lookin' at the boat, you touched me on my back and you feeled me up. You want to fuck fuck on the ocean, don't you? Chuck at the H&H told me you asked about me. And what you asked about. He said you gave him money— lots of money—to tell you about my dick and to point me out."

Pamela reached her hand over and gently laid it on Luther's arm. "Yes, dear boy, we want to fuck you on the ocean. How wonderfully refreshing you are. And I'm sure we can come up with, what was it, a fuck fuck table?" She turned her head toward Jonathan and said, "We can find a fuck fuck table, can't we darling? Perhaps you can tell us what one looks like, Luther, dear."

After he described the table in the workshop, Luther asked Pamela, "You want me to be your friends?"

"Do you fuck your friends, Luther?"

"Yeah, sure."

"Then, yes, Luther. Jonathan and I want to be your very good and close friends." Pamela sat back in her chair, gave a little laugh, and inclined her head to her husband.

"Well, is it true what this Chuck said about your equipment, Luther?" Jonathan asked. "Did your friend, Chuck, earn his money?"

"What? My equipment? And Chuck ain't my friend in that way. He was a before kind of friend. I don't fuck fuck with Chuck."

Pamela chuckled. "Fuck fuck with Chuck. How cute. He means your cock, sweetheart, your dick. Does it push a foot long? Is it as thick as a baseball bat? Is it darker than the rest of you? Can you fuck for a long time? Do you go off like the Fountain of Youth? Are you and we going to have a very good time? Chuck got money. If Chuck was right about your cock, you can have so much more than Chuck got. He fucked OK, but nothing special—and he couldn't keep it up—at least not to our requirements."

Luther was blushing. "You talk fast. I think I need to go the bathroom now. Is that OK?"

"But Pamela asked you—"

"Don't you need to go to the bathroom too, Jonathan dear?" Pamela asked, giving him a meaningful look.

"Yes, I guess I do," he said, standing. Luther was already on his way.

Standing at the urinals, side by side, Jonathan looked over and down—and felt weak in the knees and almost let out a gasp.

"Can . . . can I touch it?" Jonathan asked in a whisper full of awe.

"Yeah sure. Let me shake it off first."

"Oh, holy fuck," Jonathan exclaimed as it lay long and heavy in his hands. He wanted to go down on his knees and worship it. He started to mention that the stalls were empty. But then he remembered Pamela back at the table and knew she would be royally pissed of he had a first go. And Pamela pissed was not a good sight. It was her money they were living on.

Returning to the table, Jonathan was rather stumbling. He looked at Pamela and nodded imperceptibly.

"I think we need to do some shopping," Pamela said with a perky voice. "Show us where the best men's shops are, Luther."

"I think they are on the walking mall behind us," Luther answered. "But I thought you were going back to the shop."

"Maybe some other time, darling. For now, we need to get you some new clothes worthy of the yacht."

"And then we'll take you out on the ocean?" Jonathan said, wording it as a question but trying to make it an accepted statement.

"I can't today or tomorrow." Luther said.

"We really—" Jonathan responded. He was getting a little perturbed.

"I can't today. I work today. I can't tomorrow. Rob is taking me fishing tomorrow. He needs me to help him. And Tim and Alfred need me to help them at the shop today." Luther was getting a little agitated.

Pamela stepped in to smooth the corners down. "We have to go to Newport tomorrow. But we'll be back. Then you will go for a cruise on our yacht with us . . . and we'll fuck you. OK, Luther? We just talked about this and you said it was OK that we fuck you. We're your friends, right? We can fuck you silly on the ocean, right? It's just that we can't do it today or tomorrow. Because you have to work today and tomorrow. You are needed at work today and tomorrow. Right? But when you aren't needed here, when you have time off, we can fuck you, right?"

Luther pondered that. "Yeah, sure. I am needed to work today and tomorrow, though." And then he brightened up. "And when you come back maybe I will have a big ring in my cock. My friend, Keith, said that would be nice for fuck fuck. He says a doctor can do that for me on Wednesday. But then that would not be a good fuck fuck time either. Wednesday wouldn't be good. And he said it would take maybe—"

"Oh Jesus, Mary, and Joseph," Pamela exclaimed. But then, when Luther gave her a strange look, she said, "Let's go on to the shops now, Luther. While we walk you can tell Jonathan again what a fuck fuck table is. I can't wait to get one."

And as an aside to Jonathan, she whispered. "A cock ring. I really can't wait. We need to be on the move or I'm going to rape him right here on the table."

"Not before I do," Jonathan whispered back. "You haven't seen his cock."

65

* * * *

Alfred had yelled to him a lot in the afternoon. He was always where Alfred didn't want him, and Alfred yelled about where he'd gotten the clothes, and kept saying that Luther couldn't get into anything because the clothes he was wearing were white and would get dirty.

"And what's this?" Alfred said when he pulled a mere nothing in gold lamé out of a shopping bag.

"That's my new bathing suit. For the cruise."

"What cruise?"

Alfred had screamed that really, really loud. He frightened Luther, and that made Luther stubborn and withdrawn. So he just said, "My someday cruise." He didn't say more than that—although he'd already said that Pamela and Jonathan had bought him the clothes.

Alfred didn't believe that much either, but Tim kept pulling him aside and saying, "Not now, Alfred. We're skating on thin ice here. We don't want to get into anything more complicated. We have to discuss this when we get home." And Tim put everything back in the bags.

Luther was glad they hadn't taken the bathing suit, although Tim had looked at it real close. Luther thought it was nice. It had a sock that his dick and balls fit in—well, mostly. Lots of the root of his cock showed because it didn't all fit inside the sock—and who knows how it would fit if he was hard. And it had strings that tied around his waist and went through his butt crack. Luther remembered Pamela had really liked that bathing suit—she was the one who said he had to have it. She had wanted to fuck fuck in the dressing room, but Jonathan said that if he couldn't do it in the restaurant bathroom, she couldn't do it in the clothing shop.

Alfred got so angry that Tim told Luther to go on home.

He was walking up Hughes street toward home, when he heard a woman's voice call out.

"Oh, there you are, Luther. Right on time."

Luther stopped in his tracks. He could see that it was Mrs. Sims calling to him. She was on the front porch of a house. But he didn't know what she meant.

"Right on time, Luther. You remembered. It's just past 3:30. Thank you for coming by to help hang those drapes and put those boxes up. You did remember, didn't you?"

"Yeah sure," Luther said. He wasn't real sure what he was supposed to be remembering. He was glad Mrs. Sims was smiling at him. Alfred hadn't been smiling all afternoon and even Tim had looked worried about something. Mrs. Sims was a good friend.

Yes, he thought, Mrs. Sims had always been a friend—one of his before friends.

"Come on into the house. My how nice you look. But are those new clothes? And oh so white."

She drew him into a living room, which was pretty and had a lot of those things in it that were in the rooms at the shop that Alfred wouldn't let him go into. What really caught his attention, though, was in front of the sofa. How strange to have that in here, Luther thought. But maybe not so strange. This was Mr. and Mrs. Sims's house. And Mr. Sims was a friend and Mrs. Sims was a before friend and probably was a special friend to her husband.

"Come through here, please, Luther. The drapes go up in the dining room. Oh, but look how dusty everything is. You'll get those nice new clothes dirty. Oh my."

"I could take them off, Mrs. Sims," Luther said.

She gave him a look of disbelief, and then she remembered who she was working with here. He was so innocent.

"Well, that would be fine, Luther. We can fold them and put them right over here on this chair." Her hands were trembling when she took the clothes. She could hardly speak. His magnificent body, only in briefs now, took her breath away.

"Here, this goes up there, Luther. Be careful now."

"It's OK, I'm good with my hands."

Oh, god, I hope so, Mrs. Sims thought. Could she really go through with this? Was this going to be as easy as it seemed? She hyperventilated as she watched him from behind, his back and leg muscles undulating, already making her wet. She wanted him so badly when he was her student. She'd almost risked her career to make a try for him then.

"OK, now the boxes, and then we'll sit in the kitchen and have some lemonade and cookies."

Luther was sitting in a kitchen chair in front of the table, when she came back with her purse. He was drinking his lemonade and looking out through the dining room to the living room.

"Now, let's see what would be a good—" she said, snapping her purse open.

"Oh, don't pay me or nothin', Mrs. Sims. We're friends."

"And you do this for your friends?" Mrs. Sims asked, a smile on her face.

"Yeah sure, I do my friends," Luther answered. He gave her a funny look.

Mrs. Sims was an English teacher. She knew what he was saying—or at least what she wanted him to be saying. She struggled with herself for a moment, but then she pulled a folded piece of paper out of her purse, unfolded it, placed it on the table in front of Luther, and stood behind him, putting her hands on his bare shoulders. Her hands were trembling.

"This is what you drew in church on Sunday and gave to me, Luther. Is there a reason you gave this to me?"

"Yeah sure, you're my friend." And you asked for it, Luther thought. But she would know that, so he didn't remind her of it. His mother had told him never to treat anyone like a dummy, especially if he didn't want to be treated like one. Also, he had forgotten Mrs. Sims wanted him to stop by in the afternoon, which he now remembered—between 3:00 and, uh, sometime— so he didn't want to be talking about remembering stuff.

"And do you know what you were drawing when you drew that? Not the secretary. It's very nice, yes. No, the other thing you drew."

"I forgot," Luther said.

She had let her hands slide down to cover his pecs. He wasn't reacting.

"But you remember now?"

Oh, fuck, Luther thought. She's going to ask me if I forgot I was supposed to come here in the afternoon. "Yes ma'am."

"What is it, Luther?"

"It's a dick."

"Is it your . . . dick . . . Luther?"

"Maybe. I don't know. I ran out of paper. It should have been longer."

Mrs. Sims drew her breath in sharply. "May I see it, Luther? Your . . . dick?"

"You want to fuck fuck with me?"

"What? What did you say?"

70

"You want to fuck fuck with me? You have a fuck fuck table."

"A what?" She followed the line of where his arm was pointing. "Oh, that tea table in the living room? Tea tables are higher than a coffee table but lower than a kitchen table. We use them for . . ." She stopped. She'd been right there, and now she was being stupid and going off the critical point.

"Oh, I thought—"

"Yes, Luther. You're right. We only call it that to friends. Yes, that's a fuck fuck table. And I'd love for you to fuck me on it, yes."

"I can fuck friends. Keith told me Tim said it was OK. And specially if there was a fuck fuck table."

Mrs. Sims was initially afraid the legs on the table wouldn't take their weight. But it was only hers, really. She was on her back and Luther stood between her thighs and fucked her. She had had to move his cock away from her anus at first, telling him, "Maybe later, dear," and then she'd had to hold the root of his cock and help him to slowly feed it in and in and in—and she had to pay attention to her clit herself—but other than that, he knew how to establish a rhythm, and she panted and moaned her way through the thickest and deepest cocking she'd ever had in her life—and she'd tried a variety of men, being just as willing to do so as she knew her husband was.

As he fucked, Luther was patting her breasts gently back and forth and giggling.

"You can suck them—the nipples—Luther," she murmured between groans. "They will like that." She cradled his head in her hands and lowered it to her breasts. He sucked on them expertly while she felt herself building and building on waves to heaven. She clutched his shoulder blades with her hands and then down to his butt cheeks, holding him close inside her. She was writhing and panting shallowly and seeing fireworks— and exploding. She collapsed under him.

"Are we done?" Luther asked.

"Not unless you want to be done, Luther."

"I like the other hole."

"We can try, Luther."

At 5:00, while they were standing on the steps, Mrs. Sims looking up the street, expecting Mr. Sims back at any moment, she went for broke.

"I have other chores needing done. Can you come back next week?"

"To fuck fuck too?"

"Yes, please."

"Maybe not next week. My friend, Keith, he said I could have a big ring put in my dickhead. Maybe this Wednesday. Next week maybe I won't feel like—"

"Oh, good lord," she exclaimed, almost fainting away on the porch. But she recovered enough to weakly say, "Well, when you've healed then. I'd like that. I'd like that very much."

* * * *

"So, you see, Luther, you need to be very careful. You need to be very careful who you have at the workshop, and you need to be extra careful when the social worker comes to talk to you. We tried to talk him out of a home visit. You aren't a child. You're an adult. But he said he also had jurisdiction for people who were, well . . . Anyway you need to be careful." Tim had run out of steam.

"I don't know why he has to make a visit here. I called the office and they said that wasn't usual," Alfred groused.

"Well, you know Mrs. Watson," Tim resumed. "She probably has been bugging them for weeks. Hasn't said boo to us, though, the witch."

"Well, you know what she's been passing around about us too, Tim," Alfred said.

Luther just sat there, at Tim and Alfred's dining room table, looking from one to the other. No, he didn't understand.

"So do you see that, Luther?" Tim asked.

"Yeah sure," Luther answered. The knitting of his brow showed the two men that he hadn't understood a word.

73

"Geez," Alfred exclaimed, exasperated.

"Now, Alfred," Time said, laying a limp hand on his arm. "This isn't helping."

He turned to Luther. "The problem is, Luther, that the man who is coming to talk to you tomorrow can send you to a school, far from here. And you'd have to live there, not here. He can do that even at your age. You need to be very polite to him, but you shouldn't say much at all about anything but your work at the shop and how much you like it there. You should say that when you're not working, you are in your room reading—and practicing your furniture making. You can tell him whatever you want about your work with furniture. Show him your drawings. Spend a lot of time showing him your drawings."

"I should show him the fu—"

"Yes, showing him the furniture in the workshop and your drawings would be very nice. Make him your friend," Alfred chimed in.

"Ah, you want me to make him my friend?"

"Yes, that would help a lot," Tim said. "And if customers come over or you have other friends come, take them the other way around the house. Don't bring them up the driveway."

"Don't bring them up the driveway?"

"No. And keep an eye out for Mrs. Watson, looking at what you're doing from her house."

"Mrs. Watson?"

74

"Yes, she's the troublemaker. She's even reported that the visits here by Mr. Sims are suspicious—when we're refinishing furniture for him here."

"Mr. Sims? He's a friend. We use the table, the fu—"

"Are you working on his table?" Alfred asked. "You've finished with the chairs already?"

"Yes, I work him on the table," Luther said. "He's nice. He's a friend."

"That's nice," Tim said, "by all means keep doing what you're doing for him. But it's getting late. We should go upstairs now. We want you to come upstairs with us tonight, Luther."

"Yeah sure."

Alfred was first. He liked to be fucked on all fours on the braided rug beside his and Tim's bed. He wanted Luther to cover him like a dog, and he like to yap like a dog when he was being fucked. When they were fucking like this, Alfred reminded Luther of a Pomeranian, even though he couldn't pronounce that name. But he'd seen one in the antique store one day, with a big, fat, old lady, and he thought that was exactly like Alfred acted when he was fucking him on the braided rug. Alfred's tongue would be out and he'd be panting, just like one of those Pomeranian dogs.

This was the best way Luther liked Alfred. When Luther was riding Alfred's ass, Alfred wasn't nasty or screaming with him. He whimpered like a dog and asked Luther to be good to him.

When Luther was pumping him deep was when Alfred said Luther was being good to him.

Tim, now, he came later. Tonight, after Luther had filled Alfred's insides, and Alfred had stopped barking, they got up off the floor and Alfred told Luther to lay down on his back on the bed.

A few minutes later Tim came in. His hair was down and he had bright red lipstick on. He was wearing a brassiere and a lady's taupe-colored satin slip. He had on a garter belt and stockings, but no panties.

All Tim ever wanted Luther to do was to lay on his back on the bed, grasp the brass headboard above his head with his hands, and stay hard. Tim would kiss him all over his body, leaving red lipstick marks, and then he would mount Luther's cock and ride him until Luther ejaculated.

For this, Tim and Alfred gave Luther a home and a semblance of a job, and would protect him as well as they could from the rest of the world—and from the predators they knew were out there. Well, the *other* predators.

When Tim was finished with Luther's cock, he climbed off and murmured with a thick voice, "Where is that gold bathing suit you bought today, Luther?"

"Downstairs, in the bags," Luther answered. "I didn't put the stuff away, I'm sorry. It's still in the bags. Downstairs. I stopped at the house before going to my room, and, I just left . . ."

"Could you go get that bathing suit and put it on for us? And, Alfred, could you go find the camera?"

* * * *

When Luther left them later in the evening, Tim and Alfred where stretched out against each other on the bed in a 69 position, not paying a bit of attention to Luther. This was how he usually left them, and he had no idea what they did afterward— nor did he have any curiosity what that was.

He padded downstairs in his new bathing suit, gathered up his bags of clothes Pamela and Jonathan had purchased for him, and went to his room behind the workshop. Luck was with him; this was the time for one of Mrs. Watson's favorite television shows that she had to watch in her parlor on the other side of her house.

CHAPTER FOUR: NOT AS DOPEY AS YOU THINK

The refrigerator door slammed shut with an uncharacteristic crack, and Cliff could hear something falling inside.

"Oh, fuck."

He knew he should open it and survey the damage, but he didn't have the time. And he didn't have the inclination. He was royally pissed.

Zack hadn't come home the previous night.

This wasn't the first time this had happened. Zack was too cocky. He thought too much of that big black cock of his—assuming too much of its control over Cliff. But that wasn't what really pissed Cliff off. What really pissed him off was that he knew he was lying—that he was, in fact, letting Zack lead him around by that big, black cock of his. His was pissed because Zack wasn't inside him right now.

Cliff pushed the stop button on the coffee machine—or at least thought he had. The blue light was still on. He reached over and jerked the plug out of the wall.

"Fixed that," he growled. And indeed he had. No lights were showing now, and he'd tried to stop it too fast. There was no coffee in the slot either.

"Fuck it," he said and sat at the kitchen island and stuffed the dry toast in his mouth.

He was conflicted. Despite wanting Zack to be fucking him now, Cliff was getting to where he didn't want Zack at him so much of the time—or at least that's what he had thought he felt. Now that Zack had been out all night, Cliff had accepted that he'd become addicted to big, black cock. And a lot of it.

Well, he had to pull himself together. He had to go see that Waters boy today and determine whether he was the menace to society that that old bitty, Mrs. Watson, had testified to. But Waters wasn't really a boy. He was a young man. And his employers had declared that he was a good worker and was quiet and decent.

Cliff snorted at that, though. Those two fairies? he thought. With what Mrs. Watson was alluding to, having the guy working and living with them might be just the reason he needed to be bundled off to a school where they helped the slow, as his regulations now said he had to refer to it. Just how slow was he, though? Cliff wondered.

Well, he thought, as he stood up from the island counter and sighed. That's what Cliff was supposed to determine by visiting him today.

As Cliff was getting into his car, he looked up at the entrance to his apartment house and saw Zack entering it. But Zack wasn't alone. There was a young white guy with him—and Zack was guiding him toward the apartment entrance with the palm of a hand cupping the young man's butt cheek.

"Shit!" Cliff exclaimed to the steering wheel and slammed his car door hard. He's going to fuck him in my bed, I'll bet. Waited for me to leave and then couldn't wait to get him upstairs in my bed. Well, we'll see about that when I get back this evening.

As he walked down the driveway between the white Victorian house on Washington Street and Mrs. Watson's house—obviously the complaining bitty's house, because he saw her peeking out of her kitchen window—Cliff was still thinking about both having to throw Zack out, which he knew he'd have to do, and wondering whether he could get along without Zack's big, black cock, which he also knew wasn't likely.

He knocked on the door to the building at the end of the driveway, and nearly dropped his jaw when it was answered by the most beautiful, hunky young man dressed only in a gold sock bathing suit that didn't contain everything it was supposed to. He'd seen the guy briefly at the antique store earlier in the week, but he hadn't registered then as the hunk that he exhibited now. Of course, he was wearing clothes then.

"Hi? You the social worker guy?" Luther asked, with a big smile on his face.

"Yes, yes, Cliff Trent. But let's go inside." He pressed his hand against the chest of the young hunk to move him out of the doorway. A zap of screaming nerves went through his body at the feel of the hard flesh. While he was pushing, he was looking around, trying to see if they could be viewed by Mrs. Watson from her kitchen window. He didn't think so.

Luther had retreated backward. "You OK?" he asked.

"Yes, yes, of course. I just didn't expect . . . What are you're wearing?"

"You don't like it? Pamela and Jonathan bought it for me. To go riding them in their yacht. But if you don't like it, I can . . ."

"No, no . . . oh, sweet crap . . . oh, oh. Is that all yours?"

Luther had gone ahead and stripped off the sock. Cliff feel on his knees in front of him.

"Oh, god, oh, god. I've got . . ." he had taken Luther's cock in his hands—lovingly—and was rubbing it on his cheeks. "Oh god. Big. Black. The biggest I've . . . oh, my."

"Tim and Alfred told me to be nice to you. They said you wanted to be my friend. If you like we can fuck fuck on my table over other. Tim told me to use it."

"Ummm, ummm," was all Cliff could manage. He already was trying to stuff as much of the cock in his mouth as possible.

Luther fucked him from behind, bent over Luther's special table. Luther was holding Cliff in place with a hand palming his belly and the other cupping his throat, pulling his head back onto Luther's shoulder.

"Oh shit, oh fuck, oh, god, yes," Cliff was stroking his own cock with one hand, palming Luther's butt cheek behind him with the other, and whimpering as Luther pumped his cock up into him from behind.

"You like to fuck fuck with me?"

"Oh, god, yes. But do you know what would be the best?"

"No, what?"

"Bound. I like to be bound when I'm fucked."

"Oh, you want to be a special friend, then? That's what Keith says when he wants to be tied up to my bed in my room. Tim said I shouldn't take anyone into my room. But Keith, he said it was OK for special friends. And Tim told me to be nice to you. You want to go into my room and fuck fuck tied up?"

"Oh fuck yes!"

* * * *

Cliff was laying on his back, his wrists tied to the rails of the brass headboard above him. Luther was sitting on his hips and idly playing with holding their cocks together and slapping them on Cliff's belly.

"So, we are friends now?" he looked down into Cliff's face and asked shyly.

"Yes, Luther we are very good friends now."

"And you will come back to work out with me on my fuck fuck table?"

"Yes, I surely will, Luther."

"And I don't have to go away to some dumb-people's school?"

"No, you don't have to go away to school, Luther."

* * * *

Luther's steps became more halting as he approached Keith's lifeguard stand on the Cape May beach that afternoon. He was coming to coordinate with Keith on his appointment the next day to have his cock glans pierced for a cock ring, and, since that would put Luther out of commission for a couple of weeks, he was hoping Keith would go back with him to the Washington Street house for a good cocking.

But Keith wasn't alone. He was standing beside his station, looking out to the ocean, but there was an older man standing there too—very close to Keith.

Luther sauntered up to them, though, and touched Keith's arm.

"Oh, hi there, big guy," Keith said. "So the Pink Poodle twins have let you free for a while?"

"I'm not working today, Keith," Luther said. He was talking to Keith, but he was looking at the man standing next to his special friend. "I wanted to talk about the doctor time tomorrow, and I thought maybe if you could come over to my house, 'cause, you know, after tomorrow . . . for a while . . ."

"This is Hamilton, Luther," Keith said, it being obvious Luther wanted to know. "Isn't he cute? He lives in South Carolina . . ."

"In Charleston," the man who Luther might say was rich looking and handsome, for a man that old, but not cute, interjected in a smooth Kentucky Bourbon voice.

". . . and he's here just for the summer. We've become good friends."

The "good friends" comment hit Luther like a ton of bricks. He knew what "good friends" meant. And as if to accentuate his distress, the man put an arm around Keith's waist and gave Luther a big smile.

"He says I can call him Ham, though. Isn't that cute?"

That disturbing "cute" crap again. "So, about tomorrow . . ."

85

"Sorry, Luther, I forgot about that. You still have the appointment, but Ham's invited me to go check out an Atlantic City casino with him. Isn't that great? He's got the most flash Jaguar convertible you've ever seen. You went with me to the doctor's office already. I'm sure you can find it and can get a ride home. Have you ever been to a casino? I haven't."

"Umm, well, OK. I gotta go now. I'm late to getting back to work."

Luther turned and walked away, leaving Keith looking a little confused. Hadn't Luther just said he had the day off? Keith thought. The tall, thin, older man of distinguished demeanor and a silky smooth southern accent voice leaned down and whispered in Keith's ear and then kissed him on the earlobe. Keith gave a little laugh and the man moved his hand to Keith's butt cheek and squeezed it.

Luther went straight to the Pink Poodle antique store, where Tim and Alfred quizzed him on how the visit that morning went with the social worker.

"Great," he said. "We're good friends now."

"But did he say anything about—?" Alfred started to ask.

"He said I don't have to go away to any school. He likes me right here. We're special friends."

"Let me get this straight; did he—?"

"Let it go, Alfred," Tim interceded. "He said the social worker isn't sending him away. We told Luther he should try for this result. Let's not worry how he did it."

Luther then asked if there was anything he could do here, but Tim told him to go home and get some sleep.

"You're going night fishing with Rob Leighton," he said. "You'd be good to get some sleep before you go."

Luther hadn't told Tim and Alfred about getting his cock ring on Wednesday—he thought they'd just fret. And maybe even tell him he couldn't. But he might have to ask them about taking him home from there. Now that Keith couldn't. Now that Keith had a new friend. Luther wondered if that meant Keith wasn't his special friend any more.

He trudged home, waving to Mrs. Watson's ruffling curtains as he passed her kitchen window, and went directly to his bed, where he lay and worried about Keith, and masturbated himself into a troubled nap.

* * * *

"There, I think that sets all of the nets, lines, and pots. Now is the time for patience. A good four hours, I think. I will go below." Rob stood there, looking in some purposeful way at Luther for a good ten seconds.

Luther looked over at Rob and smiled while he was being scrutinized. He was sitting on a padded bench on the port side of the well of the boat and watching the last fingers of red, orange, and purple light of the sunset. It made him think of the night Keith and he had gone into the water off the Cape May beach and fucked as the lights of the town flickered on for the evening. The thought of this made him sad.

He was thinking too of the next day—getting the cock ring put in. He hadn't thought before of the possible pain of having that done. But now, when Keith wasn't going to be there with him, he was beginning to think he should have given this more thought. Still, though, Pamela had said she wanted to fuck fuck with it. And Jonathan too. They'd bought him some clothes to wear when they went out on the yacht. He didn't want to disappoint them.

"So, I'm going below now," Rob repeated. "I'll take a shower."

"Yeah sure," Luther said, and then he turned his face back to the sunset.

Then Rob turned and clumped down the steep stairway in the hatchway to the cabin below.

The sea was calm, and there was very little pitching. Luther felt his body moving in rhythm with the rise and fall of the boat on the waves moving in toward the Jersey shore.

Luther sat and watched the distant shoreline for about a half hour. Then he stood and stripped off the shorts and briefs he'd been wearing, moved to the hatch to the cabin below, and descended.

It was almost totally dark in the cabin, but he'd been here several times before and he knew what was where.

He could hear the heavy breathing, and he moved around to the left in the cabin, making sure he didn't upset anything and thus reveal where he was. The breathing was to his right now.

He turned and lunged, extending his arms. He encountered man flesh. Rob yelped in the dark, as Luther embraced his body and pulled him in. The two began to struggle in the dark, to wrestle on the floor of the bobbing boat, set in a rolling motion by the lurching and grasping and lunging of the two strong bodies.

Slowly, though, ever so slowly, Rob gave way to the strength and superior wrestling prowess of the younger man. Luther trapped Rob's body below his on the floor. Rob was panting and moaning his exhaustion. Luther stood, his feet straddling Rob's hips. He leaned down, scooped his arms around Rob's belly, and pulled his torso off the floor. Rob was so exhausted he dangled there between Luther's legs, his head hanging down, his arms swaying with the movement of the boat, the tops of his feet resting on the decking.

Luther started working his cock inside Rob's channel, and the older man groaned and burbled a reaction that could either be begging for relief or moaning for the fuck. Rob whimpered and groaned and spilled his seed on the deck between Luther's feet as Luther slow pumped him to his own ejaculation.

Shortly thereafter, Rob was laying, in the dark, on his belly on the bunk, his wrists tied to the headboard, and his legs bent up with restraints on his ankles attached to the bottom of the bunk overhead. He was babbling and sobbing once again as Luther straddled his hips and rode his ass to another ejaculation by each.

Afterward, Rob no longer bound, the two lay on their sides on the bunk, Rob cuddled inside Luther's lap.

"God, it seemed like an eternity before we could get out here," Rob murmured.

"You liked the fucking?"

"I always like your fucking, Luther."

"But still we have to do it in the dark, and you make me fight you for it and tie you up."

"Yes, Luther. You know how I feel about that. The guilt. I want it—oh shit how I want this big cock of yours—but I can't do it without the feeling that it's been taken from me and I can't do anything about it. And it must be in the dark. I can't be seen in the dark. It's not really happening if it's in the dark."

"I like fucking you. You were one of my first fuck friends. Tim told me I should only do it with him and Alfred. But you were one of my first fuck friends before I went with Tim and Alfred. So you don't count."

"One of your first fuck friends?"

"Yeah sure. You and Father Paul."

"Ah, Father Paul. Do you and Father Paul . . .?"

"No, Not any more. He said he has to be very careful."

"Luther. Do you ever feel like you want to get away from Cape May?"

"Get away? Why?"

"I know that people take advantage of you here—and that they treat you like you were a dummy."

"The joke is on them then, isn't it, Rob? I'm slow, but I'm not a dummy."

"No, Luther, you're not a dummy. I've known you for so long, been close to you for so long. But taking advantage of you . . ."

"You think you are taking advantage of me? Who do you think started our fuckings? Did you think you were taking advantage of me?"

"Well, yes, a little."

Luther laughed. "I picked you, Rob, I wanted to fuck you. I pick them all. A little dummy talk, and they think they are fooling me. But they are fooling me to do what I want to do with them. I fuck and people give me what I want. Leave Cape May? No, I have everything I want here."

"Who do you fuck, Luther?"

"Anyone I want. They see my cock, and they lay down and open their legs to me. They beg me to fuck them."

"I certainly did, didn't I? But women. I know you fuck men, but women? Do you fuck them too?"

"Yeah sure. They have holes, don't they? I like them, I fuck them."

"And the girls; do you fuck them too?"

"No, not girls—or boys either. Too dangerous. I want to stay in Cape May."

"You certainly are no dummy, Luther." Rob made the mental note to keep fighting Madge off on Luther being a danger to their girls or anyone else's. He believed Luther. Luther acted differently when the two of them were alone; he believed that Luther laid it on thicker than reality in public. "You said Cape May has everything you want. Everything? You don't want riches and all of the good things in life?"

Luther laughed again. "Well, tomorrow I'm having a cock ring put in my dickhead. Then I'll have everything I want. Cape May gives me everything I need or want."

Rob shuddered within Luther's embrace. "A cock ring?"

"Yes, a big, thick, silver one—to go with my big, thick dick."

"Oh, god, Luther, you're going to make me come again."

"OK, if you want."

92

The next twenty minutes featured no talking. Luther was side splitting Rob from behind and stroking his cock until Rob cried and came for him once again—safely in the dark.

"That cock ring, Luther. Can I be the first one to feel it inside me?"

"If you want. You're my first real friend—I don't think Father Paul is a real friend He's so nice, nice. But not a real nice."

"I'll be happy to pay for it, Luther—the cock ring operation. And, if you don't have anyone else to take you to the doctor's and then to take you home, I'll do it."

"Thank you, Rob. You're a special friend."

"But you'll let me be the first you use it with, won't you?"

"Yeah, sure, you're a special friend."

Luther smiled in the dark, knowing that Rob didn't know what a special friend was to him, already imagining them in his bed, Rob bound, the lights off, the bed groaning and bouncing up and down, and Luther punishing Rob's channel deep with the feel of his new cock ring.

And that concern was put to rest too. Not only was someone going to be with him for the operation and to take him home, but he was going to pay for it too. All of those people just didn't get it. They thought they were taking advantage of him, when they were providing him everything he wanted and needed. All because they wanted his big, black cock inside them. Luther didn't know his daddy, but he thanked him almost every night for the big, black cock.

CHAPTER FIVE: WHAT'S THE MOST IMPORTANT?

Rob wasn't gasping at the effect of the cock ring anymore, but he was showing how much pleasure it was giving him still when Luther played it on his prostate, by grasping the brass rails of the headboard overhead to which his wrists were bound and pulling his feet away from the baseboard to which his ankles were bound enough to dig his heels into the bedspread and raise his pelvis to the perfect angle for Luther to drag the cock ring across the prostate again and again and again.

Rob threw his head back and mouthed a silent scream of ecstasy as he shot his load. It was a weak spurt this time, but it had been the third time. Each prolonged visit of the cock ring to the prostate had caused him to ejaculate. His balls ached from the frequent demands on them, but each time he had been aroused to glorious heights.

Luther sank his cock deep again. "Bouncy, Bouncy, Squeak, Squeak," he chortled as he made the bed springs sing for him in his hard, deep pounding. Then he too was throwing his head back and yowling, ejaculated, and collapsed on top of the older man.

"Like my new dickhead?" He whispered, as he embraced Rob closely in the dark room.

"Oh, god, yes, I like it just fine."

"I promised you'd be the first one. And you are. I like it too. I can feel that you really like it. That makes me happy."

"I'm glad I'm the first. It's a great gift, Luther."

"You paid for it."

"And it's worth every penny. I'll come any time you call me, Luther. I'm lost to you. I'm leaving my cell phone number and anytime you want me, just . . . Oh, holy shit!"

Luther had drawn the cock out to just inside Rob's entrance again and was dragging the cock ring across his prostate for a fourth time. Rob dug in his heels and raised his pelvis to give Luther the perfect angle. And he cried out in ecstasy as the metal ring dragged across his prostate again and again and again, sending him into orbit. His pelvis shuddered and his cock fired off—blanks this time, as there was no more cum inside him. But beyond the dull ache in his balls, he still saw and felt the fireworks.

* * * *

It had gone well with Rob. Very well. Luther couldn't wait to try it with Keith. After lunch he walked as fast as he could to the Cape May beach.

"It's Keith's day off. He's probably at home," Luther was told.

Luther knew where Keith lived—in a converted garage behind a bungalow on Fow Avenue, out toward the marshes on the town's west end. He walked over there from the beach. He hadn't seen Keith since before he got his cock ring. They always wanted to fuck when they saw each other, and Luther didn't want to have the tension between them if he couldn't fuck. But he knew that would just make it better for both of them when Luther had his new cock ring and could use it.

He slowed his pace as he turned off Grant onto Fow. There was a fancy car parked up there near Keith's place. Luther didn't know what it was until he got close enough to read the writing on the car, but he really knew it was a Jaguar before he got there. He walked slowly down the bungalow's driveway, and, not wanting to embarrass himself, he went around to the side of the small building and looked in the window before knocking at the door.

Keith was inside, in an upholstered chair—but not in the chair the way a normal person would sit. He was reversed, with his shoulders on the front edge and his head and arms arched back toward the floor. His legs were raised and spread above the back of the chair. The older, rich-looking guy Keith had introduced as Ham from Charleston, South Carolina, was standing on a stool behind the chair, holding Keith's legs spread with his hands gripping Keith's ankles, and fucking down into Keith with a long, long thin cock.

Luther's hand involuntarily went down to his own basket. He was a lot thicker, but he might not be much longer than this guy. Each time the cock went in all the way, the man took the root between two fingers and revolved it in Keith's hole. Luther could hear the cries of Keith's ecstasy and passion through the window. Luther well knew what sounds Keith made when he was being well fucked. He watched with added disappointment when he saw Ham's cock come all of the way out of Keith's hole. He had a big cock ring in the head—just like Luther now had.

Luther's wouldn't be anything new for Keith.

Luther couldn't take his eyes away from the tableau. Keith was in a position Luther had never seen—or even imagined—before. He wanted to fuck Keith that way too. He was struck by what a small, light figure Keith was, although well-muscled in his compact package, when the old man leaned down and pulled Keith out of the chair, gathered him in his arms, and walked him over to a bed. He laid Keith down on his back, with one leg descending to the floor and the other one running up the tall, thin man's chest. Ham fucked Keith in long, long slides while Keith arched his back and moaned. He then turned Keith onto his belly, rotating him on the buried cock, and continued fucking him from behind.

Then Ham had his cock half way out, taking slow slides, and Luther could tell that he was punishing Keith's prostate with the cock ring. He could tell that because Keith was making the same ultimate-pleasure sounds that Rob had made for Luther when Luther was practicing on Rob the gift he had wanted to give Keith himself. Luther had wanted to be the first to give this gift to Keith because it had been Keith's idea that he get a cock ring. Keith raised his pelvis to give Ham just the right angle on his prostate and then, with Ham holding his waist firmly in his hands, Keith was writhing and crying out—and ejaculating up onto Ham's belly. Ham kept on fucking; not bad stamina for a man that old, Luther thought, not wanting to admire him but unable to be unfair about it.

When Luther had finally had enough and turned away, the last vision he had was of Keith's weight supported on his shoulders on the carpet at the base of the foot of the bed. His back was rising up the bed and his legs were spread wide. Ham was holding them there and fucking down into Keith's channel, again in those long, long slides.

Boy did Luther want Keith to let him fuck him in those positions. And he wanted Keith to cry out for him the way he was crying out for that old dude, Ham.

But this wasn't a day for Luther to be visiting Keith, he decided. And now he didn't wonder what Keith had been doing while waiting for Luther's cock to heal from having the cock ring piercing Keith had suggested.

Despondent and confused about whether Keith was still his special friend, Luther walked back up the driveway and down Fow Avenue. As he walked, a guy passed him on a bike. He stopped the bike and turned and looked at Luther. He was a sweet little trick, Luther thought. Small and compact, like Keith. But dark and with black curly hair on his head and on his chest and arms, unlike Keith's light blond hair. He was wearing just a Speedo and tennis shoes—probably being on his way to the beach. He smiled at Luther, and although Luther felt anything but happy, he couldn't help smiling back.

Luther wondered if the guy could put his body in interesting positions like Keith did for Ham when he was fucked. The thought made Luther go hard again, although he hadn't gone completely flaccid yet from watching Keith and Ham doing those contortions.

The young man turned on his bike and peddled away. But he was waiting for Luther at the entrance of a seaside park that led down to the ocean, with a wooden-deck walkway running between a tidal basin on one side and a stand of trees separating the park from the adjacent residential section on the other side.

He stood there, straddling his bike, and smiling as Luther approached.

"Hey, aren't you Luther Waters?" The young man asked as Luther reached him.

"Yeah sure, I am," Luther answered.

"I'm a cook at the H&H. My name is Kwame. Charlie told me about you."

"Charlie?"

"Yeah. We're alike, you and me. My dad's black and my mom's white. I thought that was a curse, but Charlie told me how it could be a good thing. He told me you're doing just fine with it."

"Me? I'm doing fine?"

"Yeah. Is it true that you have a humongous cock and it's almost black?"

"It's got a nice cock ring in it too," Luther said, with pride. "Bigger and thicker than that one in your nipple. But that's a nice one too."

"Can I see it?"

"What? Here?" Luther said. But he was already unzipping his shorts.

"No, not here, of course. There are small groves of palm trees in this park."

Luther fucked Kwame in a sandy-soil depression among a stand of sea oats under palm trees. He, like Kwame, was thrilled that they both had the cocks of black men, although Kwame was more black in other traits than Luther was and the contrast of cock color and skin tone was more pronounced in Luther than in Kwame. Kwame screamed good and egged Luther on in a very arousing way while Luther was entering him. Kwame was on his back, legs spread, and Luther covered him from above. While Kwame became used to having the cock buried deep inside him, Luther played with Kwame's nipple ring with his mouth. Then Kwame was on his shoulders with his legs stretched up and doing the splits while Luther stood over him between them and fucked sideways down into Kwame's hole in a position Luther thought Keith would like. Kwame was making noises like Keith had made for Ham, which made Luther happy.

But Luther didn't stay in that position for very long. He was fascinated by Kwame's nipple ring and moved back into a position so that he could play with that with his teeth. Kwame mumbled that he didn't care how Luther fucked him as long as he kept his cock buried and churning.

"Maybe I get me one of these too," Luther muttered.

Kwame was unable to answer. He was huffing and puffing at the effort to expand his channel to accommodate Luther's cock. His hands were pressed into Luther's buttocks.

Then Luther began to pump him in long, deep thrusts.

"Oh sheet! Fuck yes. Giv't me!"

Luther was interested to learn that Kwame reacted to the cock ring just as Rob did. When Luther brought the head of his cock out near Kwame's entrance and began dragging it back and forth over Kwame's prostate, Kwame clutched at Luther's back, shoulders, or buttocks; dug his heels in the sand; raised his pelvis to give Luther the best angle for the punishment of the prostate; threw his head back and yowled; and shot off a load.

The difference between Rob and Kwame, though, was that Kwame was younger and more virile. He shot a load five times before he begged Luther to stop because his balls ached so badly. And even when Luther did it one more time, and Kwame had collapsed in exhaustion, his cock managed one more weak discharge.

Then and only then did Luther proceed to the short pumps deep, building up to his own ejaculation.

This was what Luther had come to give Keith. It was nice that there was someone he could give it to.

"Do you like being my fuck fuck friend?" Luther asked as they kissed afterward.

"Yes, lots," Kwame answered.

Luther beamed a smile. One more nice friend for him to play with. And one so much like himself.

"Does Charlie at the H&H fuck you?"

"Yes . . . are you gonna mind that, Luther—when you fuck me?"

"No. I think each one should enjoy whatever they can get."

That stopped him and made him think of Keith and Ham. Why wasn't he giving Keith that latitude? Did he think of Keith in a different way from how he thought of anyone else? He'd have to think about that, but now he was thinking again about what Kwame had just said.

"You mean you want to fuck fuck with me again."

"Of course. You're the best."

"Better than Charlie?"

"It's not even close. Better than anyone. And I want you to fuck me again now."

Luther laughed a happy laugh and rolled back on top of Kwame. Kwame wrapped his legs around the small of Luther's back, hooked his ankles, grabbed Luther's shoulder blades, and groaned deeply as Luther thrust inside him again and began the fuck anew.

"That thing you did on my G spot with the cock ring?" Kwame asked. "Can you do that again? That was some serious shit."

* * * *

The next afternoon Luther was working at the Pink Poodle and mostly being asked not to meddle with this and that by an agitated Alfred, whose agitation, however was somewhat subdued today. He'd been fucked gloriously with a cock ring the previous evening.

Luther looked up at the hailing of his name and came face to face with Keith.

"Can we talk, Luther?"

"Yeah sure," Luther said, turning a neutral gaze on Keith. "So, talk."

"Someplace private maybe? I saw you looking through my window yesterday, Luther. Can we talk someplace private?"

"OK, there's a furniture storeroom back here."

"I want to explain, Luther. What you saw yesterday. Ham wants to take me back to Charleston. He's rich, Luther."

Luther had him backed up to a table edge. Luther was fisting the edge of the table on either side of him.

"Don't be mad, Luther. You know me. You went a couple of weeks without being with me. Ham came along at a special time. That's all. He's good to me. Look, he bought me this watch."

"Look at my watch, Keith. Pamela and Jonathan bought me that. It didn't stop me from fuck fucking you the next day."

"And he said he could get me transferred to a good design school down in Savannah. He'd pay for it all."

"Can he fuck fuck like I can?"

"He's good; he's very good. And he's got a cock that—"

"Yes I saw his cock," Luther growled. "And I saw that he was good—for his age."

Keith's answer had been delivered with a toss of his head and an expression of defensive challenge. That inflamed Luther rather than calmed him down. He lifted a surprised Keith onto his butt on the table top, grabbed for the waistband of his shorts, and stripped his shorts and briefs off his legs before Keith could react.

"No, Luther . . . no, please . . . shit . . . fuck. Oh, god!"

"Feel me? You make me hard. We're special friends. This is what I want. This is what you said you wanted."

With each sentence he had thrust his cock further up into Keith's channel. He was embracing Keith's chest in a choke hold, as if he could not let his friend escape.

"Oh, Luther . . . Oh, Luther . . . Oh Shit!"

Luther had brought his cock head out to where he started dragging it across Keith's prostate. Keith threw his head back, laid in Luther's embrace, and let his arms dangle at his side. He dug the heels of his deck loafers into the rung running under the table and lifted his pelvis to give Luther just the right angle for punishing the prostate. He panted and whimpered and, after several minutes gave a jerk and a little cry and ejaculated up Luther's belly.

"Am I the best?" Luther challenged. "Better than Ham?"

"Yes, you are the best, Luther."

He managed to sit upright on the table. "But you aren't forever, Luther. Neither am I. I have to get what I can now. You do too. You need to believe that. I have to go to Charleston with Ham—for as long as he will have me and give me things. I won't be young and desirable forever. Neither will you. Thank about it."

Luther paused for a moment and then he said, in a very serious voice, "But I give the best fuck fuck, don't I?"

"Yes, Luther. You give the very best . . . oh, fuck!"

The cock ring was punishing his prostate again. With a moan and a sigh, Keith laid back in Luther's arms, dug his heels into the rung under the table, raised his pelvis to the desirable angle, moaned and groaned for a few minutes, and shot another load.

Then he groaned and grunted his way to Luther pumping him hard for his own release.

* * * *

"See, darling. There's the table you wanted, right there in the fantail. After dinner we'll give it a spin."

"Yeah, that's a fuck fuck table," Luther said. "The padded top is nice."

"Let me show you where you can change. The gold sock bikini we bought you, please. And then you sit out here on the fantail and watch us pull out of the harbor. Jonathan is up with the captain. I have a date in the lounge with a martini."

Luther had known that Pamela and Jonathan were back in the Cape May harbor for several days. He had initially planned to ignore that. But two things worked at his mind and caused him to appear and tell Pamela and Jonathan that he was ready to take that cruise on the ocean to go out and fuck them. Both thoughts came out of his last encounter with Keith. Keith had been so passionate about wanting to grasp the golden ring while he still could. The argument for that wasn't totally lost on Luther. And Keith had caused Luther to point to the very nice watch Pamela and Jonathan had bought for him. They had bought him clothes too— clothes to go on a cruise. He owed them. He didn't want to start taking things for free. They wanted to be fucked in payment for their gifts. If all he needed to do was go out on the ocean with them for a day and fuck them, he would give them what they wanted for the nice things they had given him. Hadn't Jonathan offered him $1,000 for the use of his cock? Surely what they had given him wasn't worth that much.

Besides, he liked Pamela and Jonathan. They were his friends. They were honest with him. They told him exactly what they wanted. He thought that was sexy. And they were both very good looking.

The yacht hadn't even cleared sight of the harbor when Pamela, perched on a bar stool at the bar in the lounge, almost spilled her martini. She could hear her husband screaming bloody murder.

She sauntered more than rushed out to the doorway to the fantail. Jonathan was belly down on the fuck fuck table, his arms stretched out wide over his head, clutching at the rim of the table on the other side, and his swimming trunks were down around his ankles.

Luther was standing close behind him, clutching his hips and fucking him in long, deep strokes. He was naked; his gold sock bikini was laying on the deck beside him.

"God, it's glorious, Pam," Jonathan sang out. "The cock ring . . . you (pant, pant) . . . wouldn't believe. And the cock. God. The biggest I've ever . . . Oh, FUCK!"

The yacht's captain appeared down a ladder almost as soon as Pamela had come out onto the deck. He was handsome and burly. Immediately behind him was an equally hunky first mate.

"It's OK, we're just playing," Pamela said in a calm voice. "Go back to the bridge. You'll both get your turn with whatever floats your boats."

She rounded on Jonathan and Luther then as the crewmen scampered back up the ladder, her voice harder and with the edge of a pout. "Get out from underneath him immediately, Jonathan. You promised I could have the first fuck."

She came over and pushed on Luther's shoulder, and the young man pulled out of Jonathan's ass and turned to the side, facing her. She looked down his body and whistled.

"Oh, manna from heaven. Is that black beauty real?"

"Yeah sure," Luther answered, confusing on his face. "That is my dick."

"Yes, you sweet horse-hung hunk, it certainly is all you. And, good god, look at that toy on the end of it."

"I'm sorry. He came here and said I looked good in the swim suit but that he wanted to look at me without the swim suit. And then he wanted to hold it. And then he wanted to suck it. And then he wanted me to put it in him. I thought you wanted me to fuck fuck on the ocean."

"Yes, I most certainly want us to fuck you on the ocean, darling. But I was promised firsties. And we're not even hardly out of the harbor yet. Here, Jonathan, you get up instantly. You, beautiful. You lay down on the table on your back. Feet on the floor, yes, just like that."

Pamela was wearing a sheer beach robe over a bikini and high heels. As Luther laid down on his back on the table in cowed response to her barked orders and Jonathan removed himself to the fantail bench, Pamela stripped off her bikini bottoms, climbed up on the table, straddled Luther's hips, and slowly, ever so slowly, accompanied by a lot of groaning and moaning, descended on Luther's cock.

"Don't move a muscle," she growled. "Just stay hard. I'll do the driving."

For several minutes, she rose and fell on Luther's cock. She crouched over him after some time of riding him with her back perfectly straight and squeezing her own breasts after tossing away her robe and bikini top and bringing the nipples to her own lips for attention. After her first orgasm she crouched over Luther's chest and stared down into his face with wild and lust-filled eyes. Her hair was brushing against Luther's chest.

"That tickles," he complained.

"No talking," she commanded between pants. "And no coming before I say you can. God, you are huge. And that cock ring . . ."

Jonathan came over behind Pamela and embraced her. His hand covered her breasts, and she turned her head to him for a deep kiss. Luther felt her being pushed forward on his cock and heard her groan, and then he sensed a change within her. He wasn't the only one inside her. Her husband was in her ass. Luther could feel him through the tissue separating her two channels. Luther wished he was in her ass himself; he liked the ass better. They were tighter. That's why he liked fucking men better than fucking women, although he did like both. And with a women he could do both. But he couldn't do it now with Pamela if Jonathan already was in there.

Pamela exploded in another orgasm.

Jonathan started pumping her. Luther felt his own juices starting to rise, and he couldn't take this laying still anymore. He sat up and wrapped his arms around them both, so that his fingers were digging in Jonathan's back. He started to pump her too. Pamela was writhing and babbling and grunting and groaning between the two men as they started to coordinate the rhythm of their pumping.

"Kiss me," Jonathan growled. His chin was on Pamela's shoulders. Luther did as he was told—when he realized that Jonathan was talking to him, not Pamela. Jonathan's lips forced his open and Jonathan was sucking his tongue. The men were pumping hard.

"Now! Now! Come for me now," Pamela screamed as her third orgasm peaked.

And they both did.

Pamela lay on the padded table beside them, still moaning quietly, as, at Jonathan's request, Luther spread the older man's legs as he lay on his back and entered his hole with his cock. There, Luther liked that better, although Jonathan wasn't as tight as most of the men Luther fucked.

Luther pumped Jonathan deep for a few minutes and then brought the cock head out to near the channel opening and dragged the cock ring across the prostate repeatedly.

"Oh, fuck yes," Jonathan moaned. He dug his heels into the decking below the low table and raised his pelvis to just the perfect angle for Luther's work on his prostate. Just a few more minutes of attention to that with the cock ring and Jonathan cried out his release and shot his seed. Holding his ankles out, Luther continued doing it again and again, as Jonathan writhed and raised his pelvis each time the cock ring visited his prostate. Jonathan ejaculated again and again and again until his balls ached and he could produce no more cum. Then and only then did Luther pump him deep to his own release.

Pamela and Jonathan used Luther unmercifully the rest of the day. After drinks on the fantail, Pamela knelt between Luther's legs and worshipped and sucked his cock.

"Geez, I'm gonna come if you keep doing that."

"Please do," she said, with a laugh.

As soon as Luther recovered, it was Jonathan's turn. Of the two, Luther decided that Jonathan gave better head. He was more in tune with what turned a man on.

Nap time was Luther fucking Pamela in the good old missionary position in the master cabin.

The difference was that most missionaries didn't have a huge, black cock, a cock ring, or the endurance of an elephant. Pamela was drifting off to an exhausted sleep after he plowed her to two more orgasms. Thus, she wasn't aware of Luther leaving the cabin in search of a head to take a piss, when she would have pointed out the cabin's own master bath behind a wall panel.

While Luther was coming back down the corridor, he decided to take a break and go out on the fantail and actually enjoy the cruise on the ocean. If all he was needed for was fucking, he could have done that with them back in Cape May, on land, he groused. He was beginning to wonder how much fucking paid for what they had given him.

En route to the fantail, though, Luther came across the cabin across the corridor from the master suite. It was a guest cabin—where Luther's clothes had been put and where he had put on the golden sock bikini. Sort of a waste, he thought—all of the clothes, not just the sock bikini—he hadn't had a stitch on since he had fucked Jonathan while they were clearing the harbor.

The door to the cabin was open, and he looked in, his attention grabbed by the moaning and hard breathing—not just of one man, but of three. Jonathan and the captain and first mate were repeating what Luther had participated in out on the fuck fuck table before drinks. Except that there was only one hole in Jonathan and the two muscled crew members were both using that one hole—at the same time.

Jonathan seemed to be enjoying it, though, so Luther walked on, wondering if Jonathan could take it if one of the cocks was his. If Luther and another guy did Jonathan, his channel wouldn't seem so loose. Luther would like that better. If Jonathan asked for it before they returned to shore tomorrow, Luther would try. But he bet that just his one cock was all Jonathan could take—maybe his cock and a few fingers. Luther had seen Ham doing that to Keith, and Keith had liked it. Maybe Jonathan would like it too—and maybe Luther would too.

Dinner was all meaningful looks from Pamela and Jonathan and sexual innuendo and double entendres—most of which went right over Luther's head, much to the amusement of the jaded pair. They had permitted Luther to dress for dinner, and the two of them were dressed to the nines. The wine flowed, and Luther felt a little tipsy when Pamela took his hand and, Jonathan trailing behind them, led him back to the master cabin.

She made quite a show of undressing Luther, and she used her mouth as much as her hands as she did so. Luther was rock solid hard when she finished, which is just the way she wanted him. Whenever he asked while on the cruise what he might do, she answered that all that was expected of him was to be rock solid hard—and to do what he was told to do. When Luther stuck it in her this time, he pushed in three fingers too and wagged his tool back and forth inside her. She sounded like she liked that a lot, so Luther decided it might be a good thing to try with Jonathan too. She liked it just as well when Luther did the same thing in her ass—and Luther liked that even better.

After dinner was movie time. Not watching them; making them. Luther fucked Pamela in the ass again, standing behind her, as she lay on her belly on the bed and shared her expressions of the taking with the camera that Jonathan held as he stood on the opposite side of the bed. Before Luther ejaculated in her ass, Jonathan came up on the bed on his knees and pointed the camera down to capture Pamela giving him a blow job.

The second act was the same as the first, but with Jonathan belly down on the bed, Luther fucking his ass with the three-finger play added, and Pamela bouncing around the room catching it all on film.

The third act was Jonathan holding the camera and filming Pamela playing with Luther's monster cock and giving him another blow job.

The three slept together, but Luther's cock wasn't put into service until the next morning. Jonathan fucked his own wife to sleep.

Late the next morning, Luther began saying he was bored and was there something he could do to help on the yacht. Yet again, though, Pamela answered that he was only needed for his cock and that his chore on the yacht was to keep that rock hard and available for whatever they asked of him.

In the afternoon, Luther asked when they would be getting back to Cape May.

"We're not going back to Cape May, darling," Pamela casually answered. "In a couple of hours we'll arrive in Newport. You'll like it there. You'll have a room of your own, and we'll give you anything you want. All we want in return is for you to remain rock hard and responsive to our wants."

"Newport? We were going back to Cape May."

"No we weren't, sweetheart. We discussed all of this. Don't you remember? You agreed to be our fuck toy. We're taking you home. We'll visit Cape May again someday."

Luther opened his mouth to contradict her. He hadn't agreed to anything like this. They hadn't talked about it. She was playing him for a dope. But was that true? Had he just not remembered it?

Looking at her amused expression caused him to shut his mouth. Of course he was a dummy. He was just what they were playing him for. It wouldn't do a bit of good to argue with them. He was out here on the ocean with them. They were in complete control. And now he knew what sort of people they were—rich and spoiled people who always got what they wanted.

Pamela looked over at him, prepared for a fight. But when he didn't offer one, she shut the magazine she was reading and leaned forward.

"Now, could you masturbate for me and make it big and rock solid again and then I'll come and sit on it."

Dutifully, Luther did so. And then Pamela did what she said she was going to do too.

When Luther could see that they were pointed into a harbor, he went back to his cabin. He changed into the clothes he'd worn on board—his own shorts and briefs and a T. And his own sandals. He folded all of the clothes Pamela and Jonathan had given him neatly and put them in a pile on the bed. He took off the watch they had given him and put it on top of the pile of clothes. Then he stood at the picture window in his cabin and watched as they came into the dock. When he felt the side of the yacht hit the dock, he pushed the picture window open, climbed out on the ledge, hopped up on the dock, and started running toward land.

* * * *

"Hello, Rob? This is Luther."

"Where the hell are you Luther? I came to your room this morning. You said I could. But you weren't there. I called Tim, and he said you hadn't come home last night—or the night before that. He's worried as hell. We all are."

"I'm in Newport."

"Newport? Newport, Rhode Island?"

"Yes, I think. It's whatever Newport you can get to from Cape May in two days on a boat. Rob . . . can you come and get me?"

"Of course I can come and get you. I'll go gas up the boat right now. Where can I find you in Newport? I know, do you think you can find the Newport Yachting Center Marina? It should be right in the center of the town there."

"I think that's where I am now."

"Good. Be there anytime from tomorrow night to noon the next day. I'm coming to get you. Do you think you can manage until then?"

"Yeah, I think I'm good."

As he was standing on the dock between the marina and a row of open-air cafés and restaurants on the land side, he saw a good-looking, muscled up, middle-aged man decked out in whites and a yachting cap giving him the eye. Luther knew that look.

"Yeah, I think I can manage just fine," Luther answered. "And Rob . . ."

"Yes, Luther?"

"When I get back to Cape May, I don't think I ever want to leave it again. And I don't want lots of money and presents. And I don't want anyone keeping me. I want what I can get on my own. And I want to fuck when I want to fuck."

Silence on the other end.

"But I want to fuck you Rob. I didn't mean I didn't want to fuck you."

"OK, great," Rob answered in a somewhat confused voice. "The important thing, though, is to get you home. I want some more use of the cock ring I paid for—when you want to exercise it, of course."

Luther hung up the pay phone and turned and smiled at the man sitting in the café.

"Thirsty?" the man called out. "I'd be happy to stand you a drink."

Luther walked over to the table and sat down next to the man, looking out onto the marina rather than across from here.

"You from here?" the man asked after a waiter had brought two beers.

"No. I'm from Cape May, New Jersey. Going back there too."

"That's a nice harbor town. You like yachts?"

"Yes, most of the time."

The man made a sweeping gesture out toward the adjacent dock. "How do you like that one right over there? That's mine."

"I like it fine."

"Would you like to take that out on the ocean for a little cruise with me?"

"Do you want me to fuck you on your boat? Is that what you are asking?"

"What?" the man said in the shock of the directness of being short circuited in what he, indeed, was trying to work his way around to asking.

"If you do, this is what I can put inside you," Luther continued. He grasped the man's hand and moved it to his cock beneath the waistbands of his shorts and briefs. "It's almost black. My fuck friends like that. Do you want to be my fuck friend? And, feel. It's got a nice, thick cock ring too. It's new. My friend, Keith, said I should get one, and so I did. My friend, Rob, got it for me. They both told me I'm the best fucker they know. And that's before I got the ring. If you take me on your boat, I'll fuck you all night if you want. And I have a new trick. Three fingers in with the cock and I move it around inside you. Pamela and Jonathan both liked that—but I liked it better with Jonathan, because men have tighter holes, although Pamela's bum was tighter than her other hole. But the boat has to stay right here—and I leave tomorrow."

"Oh, sweet jesus," the man exclaimed. Then he raised his free hand and called out in an unsteady voice, "Check please."

ABOUT THE AUTHOR

Habu is one of the pen names of a former supersonic spy jet pilot, intelligence agent, male model, movie actor, and diplomat. A wild youth in South East Asia was spent enjoying whatever sexual opportunities came his way, and much of his gay male writing is about recalling incidents from those days and inventing ones he'd perhaps have liked to experience. He now leads a very quiet and ordinary happily married family life.

An American, he is a published mainstream novelist and short story writer under another name and in another dimension of his life. He has written or cowritten (with Sabb) over 500 published short stories and nearly 100 published erotica e-books, primarily of gay fiction but also memoir, straight fiction and ménage fiction. His hand and creative writing can be seen in stories and books by habu, sr71plt, Dirk Hessian, Shabbu, and Stephen Kessel—among unrevealed others that might surprise readers. The fictionalized

GM memoir *Flying High, Diving Deep* is loosely based on his life experiences. He can be found at the adults only gay male site www.BarbarianSpy.com, which he shares with Sabb.

FOR LITERARY HEAT

Not all books listed below may currently be on release.

BOOKS BY DIRK HESSIAN

The Beautiful Way

Blue and Gray

Colonel's Treasure

Beginning of Time

Prophecy of Noto

The King's Men

Labyrinth

BOOKS BY HABU

Gay Erotica

Memoir Faction

Flying High, Diving Deep

General

Hard Knocks U

Dark Angel Sounding

Man's Man

My Neighbor's Hot Tub

Trip Money

Vortex

Clint Folsom Mysteries Compendium Volume 1

Clint Folsom Mysteries Compendium Volume 2

Grab Bag 1

Grab Bag 2

Across the Threshold

The Indian Doctor

Sailorboy
Home to Fire Island
The Sporting Life
Platres Conclave
Fetish Galore!
Choke Hold
Literary Gay Erotica
Cairo Surrender
The Handyman
Homeward Bound
Journey to Mirage
Menage Erotica
13 Ways for Halloween
Luther
The Indian Prince
BOOKS BY SHABBU
Yap, Yap
Dirty Pool
Operation Black Jade
Cigars!
Angel in the Barn
Gayly Complicated
Despoiling David
The Tree of Idleness
I Met a Man
The Interview
Rough Road to Happiness
BOOKS BY SABB
The Legend of Holleystone Grange
Surprise Encounters
She is He
Wrong Man
Loyal to his King
Barbarian Tales - Book One - Traveler's Tales
Barbarian Tales - Book Two - Journeys Begin
Barbarian Tales - Book Three - The Inheritance
Barbarian Tales - Book Four - Road to Persepolis
~